The Tub & Other Strange Tales

Jim Metzger

ISBN: 0615833845
ISBN-13: 9780615833842

To Esther

CONTENTS

PART I

WE REALLY DO HAVE A HELL OF A DEAN

Here's what I said: "When the monks reach the top of the mountain, they unwrap the body, then begin cutting it into manageable pieces." I clicked the mouse, and a photo appeared of four Tibetan Buddhist monks, all bent at the waist, all hacking away at a woman's limbs. "This is the customary spot for the sky burial, so the vultures pretty much descend right away and begin tearing at the skin." I advanced the slides. "If there are enough vultures around, they can pick a body clean in under an hour." In this photo were about a dozen of the scruffiest foul you've ever seen, gathered in a circle, ripping bits of flesh from a pair of dismembered legs. "Then, the monks have a go at her torso. Sometimes, they just slice it open with their machetes without actually dividing it into separate pieces, as you see here." When I advanced the slides this time, I paused and looked out over the lecture hall, tiered slightly, and lined with rows of padded maroon flip-chairs like the kind you might see in an old movie theater. I saw maybe seven or eight faces of the one-hundred or so in the room. The rest were angled down, presumably fixated on some kind of electronic device — an iPhone, a Blackberry, a laptop, something like that. Some of the faces were happy, others were somber or even expressionless. I'd never noticed so many heads bowed at once. Had I simply not been paying attention?

"Hello," I said, tapping the microphone.

"Hello, Professor Johnson." Sarah always sat in the first row and never addressed her electronic device during class. Sarah was cute and attentive, which encouraged me.

"Isn't this interesting?" I asked. A smattering of heads turned up. "I mean, they're cutting up this woman's body because they really believe that whatever inhabited it is now totally gone. It's just flesh and bones — you know, matter, stuff. And they're offering it back to the animals as a gift, as a way to atone for all the harm we cause them when we're alive. Isn't that cool?" A young man with his feet kicked up on the vacant seat in front of him made as if he was going to speak but instead raised his index finger, signaling that I should wait a moment. He was eating a hoagie.

"Pretty gnarly, dude," he managed finally, reaching down for a can of Red Bull. I held on for more, but he just leaned back and launched into another ambitious bite.

Then, for the very first time, I really heard it: a symphony of tapping, like the patter of light rain, maybe, or like a grove of caterpillars gnawing their way through soft spring leaves. Why hadn't I noticed this before? Now, if I had been lecturing on Malinowski or Levi-Strauss or on some arcane bit of nineteenth century anthropological theory, I suppose I would have understood. But, a selection of the some of the world's weirdest funerary rites? Really, this was as good as it got. What would it take for them to quit working their thumbs? Yodeling, maybe? Or performing one of those dead-armed Irish dance numbers? Dropping my drawers? What would it take?

There was no time to pursue these thoughts further, so I just kept advancing the slides and talking. I spoke about how some Hindus build pyres right along the Ganges and cremate their dead there, dumping the charred remains into the river; about how some indigenous peoples dig-up (bare-handed!) the bones of their deceased after all the flesh has decomposed and place them in boxes or in niches in caves; about how the Parsis in India still expose their dead atop towers for vultures to pick them clean and for the sun to bake dry whatever fleshy bits remained. I was into it, I mean really into it. I showed several video clips, too. In one, a British reporter talks about how the Parsi community in Mumbai has run into trouble recently with other residents because there are no longer enough birds to finish off a corpse. Some of these bodies lie up there for months, he said, creating an awful stench, which sent some of the rich who live downwind into an uproar.

"What's so interesting," I said after this clip, "is that social pressures are forcing religious leaders in the Parsi community to recommend cremation to keep the peace. This change has nothing at all to do with divine revelation or with some deep hidden truth. It's purely pragmatic. As a minority community in Mumbai, the Parsis either change or risk being ostracized. It's about survival, really. It's as simple as that."

As the students continued to work their thumbs and to ignore every word I said, I made an outrageous promise.

"Hello," I said, again tapping the microphone. "Hello out there."

"Hello," said Sarah.

"Next week, we have a real treat. A few members of a tribe from Belize will be right here on this stage, and they will do very interesting and shocking things! For instance, a woman will breastfeed a small monkey." I paused and moved in closer to the microphone, preparing my very best Al Green voice: "*A woman will breastfeed a small monkey.* Why? Because her people have such love for the animals that live in the forest around their village! They treat some of them like they would their own children – in fact, no differently than their own children!" I had gone too far, I had claimed too much, but I suddenly felt that getting their attention was a top priority, and that truth had shifted to second place. Sure, I had overreached, but nearly half the room's faces now were visible. Half!

Invigorated by the response, I unwisely pressed on: "We will also have small children here from a tribe in Ecuador. These children regularly venture out into the forest without their parents in search of very large and very poisonous tarantulas, which they trap with a little stick and then roast over an open fire for an afternoon snack. And they will trap and eat these spiders right here! How about that?" I imagined a spate of Oo's and Ah's, maybe even light applause, but these things didn't happen. Nevertheless, I'm happy to report that about eighty percent of faces were visible at this point.

One more vow came forth that day: "And, as if things couldn't get any better, we will have cannibals here who will crack open the skulls of enemies killed in battle and eat their brains, right here on this stage. They will wear loincloths and be very tan and carry tall spears and wear necklaces made of dried human ears! The whole thing will be as authentic as possible!" I'm happy to report that at this remark nearly one-hundred percent of faces were visible. Really, something had to be done. These students' parents were paying far too much to be bored by some talking head.

When I informed the Dean of my rash promises, she suggested I might combine my accumulated international travel allowance of $4500

5

(I hate to travel) with a portion of an unused research grant to fly in and lodge the participants. With the assistance of two TA's, I was able to make all the arrangements in just two days: the woman and monkey were scheduled for Wednesday, the small children for Friday, and the cannibals for late the following week. Because the anthropology department at State is quite large, I had no need to fly in translators: we already had faculty among us who were equipped to serve in that capacity.

On Wednesday of the next week, attendance was way up. And at first, most students seemed not to be engaging their electronic devices. This encouraged me greatly.

Naturally, I introduced the woman, explained where she was from, and thanked both her and the monkey for their willingness to come all this way on such short notice. The woman began by offering the monkey some kind of nut or bit of fruit, presumably to coax it from her shoulder into her lap. Understandably, the monkey was hesitant at first, but soon scaled down the woman's chest onto her leg. The woman slowly pulled off her shirt and held her breast out to the monkey, which immediately dropped its treat, seized hold of her nipple, and began to suck as if it had been wronged in some profound way. Nothing must have come out, because the monkey pulled back and began slapping and head-butting the breast in a most belligerent manner. I asked Professor Gilke, our translator, to ask her if she was OK, or if she would like our assistance.

"OK," she said.

The woman restrained the monkey's arms and spoke to it firmly. Almost instantaneously, it stopped behaving like a monkey and behaved more like child. She then cupped the monkey's head in her hand and brought it slowly toward her breast. The monkey placed both hands on the breast, forming a triangle around it with its thumbs and forefingers, then recommenced its ferocious sucking. There it remained for the next three or four minutes. The students were mesmerized, as I myself was too, but after the fifth minute or so had passed, heads began to drop, and the faintest pecking could be heard throughout the room.

"Ask her to rotate the monkey!" I cried. At first, the woman looked confused, but she soon began slowly turning the monkey counterclockwise until it had orbited a full 180 degrees and was feeding upside down. "How about that!" I said. Only a small fraction of heads returned to their upright position. "Can she perform a traditional dance while the monkey is feeding?" I asked. Again, the woman was confused but graciously complied with the request. The monkey very quickly grew agitated with the shimmying and the bouncing and retreated to the woman's shoulder, where it buried its face in her hair. More and more heads began to drop, so I put a stop to the demonstration and solicited questions from the class.

Q & A brought forth few questions of substance, and was a disappointment overall. Here is some of what was said:

"Why do you breastfeed monkeys?"

"Because some of the babies get abandoned by their mothers. They need milk to survive, and we can give that to them."

"Does the breastfeeding hurt?"

"Oh, yes. Can't you *see* the scars?" Many men in particular shook their heads, so the woman walked slowly down the center isle and held out both breasts for all to see. Indeed, there were multiple bite marks and unsightly skin tags around both nipples. I could see a few welts as well, presumably due to the monkey's earlier tantrum.

"What does your husband think of you breastfeeding monkeys?"

"I don't care what he thinks."

"What other animals do you breastfeed?"

"None. My aunt once tried breastfeeding a goat, but it nearly took her nipple off."

Convinced that the demonstration and Q & A would be enough to sustain a full class session, I had not prepared a lecture and therefore was forced to adjourn class early. The students seemed pleased most of all by this news. As a parting gift, the woman was given an honorarium drawn from my travel allowance as well as a coffee mug bearing our school's logo, a free year's subscription to our alumni magazine, and a set of four coasters featuring our state bird.

The tarantula-eating boys, I'm pleased to report, drew more accolades. Admittedly, the tarantulas did cause a bit of a fuss for Customs, but when officials received word that they were required to enhance the educational experience of our best and brightest and would be killed anyway, they said, "All right, but promise you'll keep those lids on tight." The boys nodded and everything was fine from that point on.

On Thursday, Jerry, head of Facilities Management and an expert carpenter, built a rectangular Plexiglass structure at the front of the classroom that resembled a child's playpen, only much larger. In the center, he created a fire pit of large stones fueled by propane. About fifteen minutes before the start of class, all of the tarantulas were released into the structure so the hunt might commence as soon as students arrived.

I expected the boys' pursuit of the spiders to involve coordinated effort and to include several edge-of-your-seat moments. But the tarantulas seemed jet-lagged and the kids were just too adept. The boys walked silently and workman-like to each of the corners of the structure, where the spiders had taken up residence. They merely compressed them against the walls with their sticks and picked them up with their bare hands. None of the spiders put up a fight. Maybe they were elderly or disabled or diseased spiders, I don't know.

Next, the boys wrapped each one in a large smooth green leaf and bound the parcels with vine so they looked like tamales. Then they rammed a pointy stick through the centers and suspended them just above the gas flame, turning them round and round while chatting amiably in their native tongue. This took about fifteen minutes. While the tarantulas were cooking, however, a lot of violent popping and fizzing issued from inside the tamales, which added some drama. I stated that the popping was probably due to rapid expansion of the spiders' joints. I couldn't be sure of the theory, but I felt it was time for something educational to be said.

As the boys were eating their charred spiders, there was quite a lot of crunching, as if they were eating pistachios but had forgotten to remove the shells. I hoped that none of the children's teeth would be damaged since there was virtually no room in the budget for dental care. I'm happy to report that none were.

Here is a very brief account of some of the things that were said during Q & A:

"What do you do with the fangs?"

"We don't eat those."

"Has anyone ever been bitten trying to catch a tarantula?"

"Yes, lots of times."

"Has anyone ever died?"

"Oh, yes. My cousin's stick broke and she got bitten and died."

"Are you afraid of the spiders?"

"No. They are slow and not very smart."

"Are tarantulas your favorite food?"

"No."

"What's your favorite food?"

"Snickers."

Again, the demonstration and follow-up proceeded more quickly than I had anticipated, leaving us with twenty or so minutes to fill. I was up late assisting Jerry with construction of the Plexiglas pen, so I hadn't time to prepare a slew of entertaining and insightful comments. Anyhow, I noticed that many students had begun to engage their electronic devices soon after the popping and fizzing had ceased. They just didn't seem much interested in watching the boys eat or in what the boys had to say afterward. The students took the news of our early adjournment well. (In addition to $1000 to be put toward the purchase of textbooks, paper, pencils, and pencil sharpeners for all the children in the village, the boys were given several bags of fun-size Snickers and inexpensive plastic toys stamped with the school's logo, which they seemed to receive enthusiastically.)

The following week, three cannibals from New Guinea arrived. The human heads, which were kept on ice and transported in large Styrofoam coolers, naturally caused quite a stir with Customs. But the very same rationale supplied for the transport of the spiders was employed in this case, and it worked just fine. Customs officials readily acknowledged that our test scores here in the States were well behind those of other industrialized nations, and that drastic measures such as these now probably are in order to bring our students up to speed. "Really," they conceded, "our future economic growth and national security depend upon it." I suppose I wouldn't have put it quite that way, but I was glad to have their support. Although the cannibals now wear t-shirts with Western logos and Lee jean-shorts, they brought along loin cloths and long sharp spears and necklaces of human ears, as I'd requested. Given that this would serve as the climactic event in the series, I felt that authenticity would be a must.

The cannibals were quite congenial, not at all fierce and aloof as I had expected. They joked around far more than I felt was appropriate for cannibals, and even had large flabby bellies not unlike the bellies of most adult Americans. They told me that they didn't really go in for cannibalism anymore, and that the heads had come not from vanquished foes but from community members who had passed recently after a bout of food poisoning ("Undercooked pork," they said).

"Then, why did you agree to do it?" I asked them.

"The money's pretty good," they said.

"Although, it could be better," one added.

"Why have you given up the practice?"

"We recently discovered that our god is a god of peace and not a god of war."

"How did you learn that?"

"Our shaman told us. Plus, our enemies now have air-conditioners and bug-zappers, which they are happy to sell us if we don't kill them."

In order to expedite the process, we placed all three heads in a convection oven and let them bake for about ninety minutes at 400 degrees so they would be ready for consumption at the start of class. I knew that if there was too much time between introducing the cannibals and eating, the students would resort to their devices and all would be lost. We also brought in a general surgeon from the hospital who had agreed to cut a 3" X 3" opening into each head with a small circular saw ordinarily used for amputations. Because the process would likely get messy, we arranged for disposable ponchos to be distributed to students in the first four rows. Although the procedure for preparing the heads admittedly was unorthodox, the cannibals were amenable overall.

The look and odor of the baked heads caused a few students to throw-up even before taking their seats, which triggered a wave of (mostly) dry heaves throughout the room. We hadn't anticipated this and lost several students right off. I was concerned about the vomit on the floor and what impact the smell would have upon the students, but I also felt that we ought to press on, given that the cannibals would be flying out later that afternoon.

The removal of the 3" x 3" squares actually went far better than expected. Blood spatter was nearly negligible since these individuals had been dead quite a while, and stray bits of flesh, bone, and hair did not make it past the first row. I'd say the cannibals took their first bite no later than 10 minutes into the class session. A few students had begun to address their electronic devices, it is true, but not so many that I became discouraged.

Watching the cannibals eat was not pleasant. They turned down our offer of forks and knives and napkins, insisting instead on using their hands, which they neither washed nor sanitized beforehand. There was a lot of tugging, ripping, and sucking of the sort you might see at a BBQ cook-off or a tailgate party, and although their table manners certainly gave the appearance of authenticity (which is what we were after), they nevertheless were a bit off-putting. I regret now not having put more thought and energy into the argument for using classic Western utensils.

About midway through the meal, I opened the floor for Q & A. Below are a few of the highlights:

"What does it taste like?"

"Like a monkey's brain."

"What does a monkey's brain taste like?"

"Like a pig's brain."

"What does a pig's brain taste like?"

"Not like a goat's brain, maybe more like a chicken's brain, which is sometimes too small to taste."

"Do you like the taste?"

"No."

"What's your favorite food, then?"

"Carmel corn. Baby Ruth. Sometimes hotdogs, but not the red shriveled ones."

"Do you always wear just loin cloths?"

"No."

"What do you wear when it gets cold?"

"Sweaters. Sometimes down jackets."

"Is it hard to kill an animal with a spear?"

"Yes, very hard."

"Who taught you how to do it?"

"No one. We don't do it. We grow yams."

The overall outcome of the conversation, as I'm sure you can see, was to raise doubts in students' minds that we had before us "real" cannibals. Some students just wagged their heads and rolled their eyes. One young man silently mouthed the words "Total fucking rip-off" just before addressing his device. One young woman turned to her friend (rudely, I thought) and whispered, "Posers." Before the cannibals had even turned their attention to the eyes — "the best part, a kind of delicacy," I said with authority – it was clear that this could no longer serve as the climactic event in our series, and that another, even more startling, would be required.

So this is what I said at the end of class: "Next week, the Dean and I will have sex right here on this stage." The Dean was equally if not more committed than I was to the education of our best and brightest, so I felt almost certain she would participate. Plus, I knew that she had spent two years after graduating from college traveling up and down the West coast in a Volkswagen bus with polyamorous nudist hippies.

"But, *why?*" moaned Sarah, clearly unhappy with the announcement. "How is that related to anthropology?"

I hadn't planned on offering a rationale. I panicked. "There is a whole sexual subculture out there – you all may know a little about it – in which people derive pleasure from pain, both from giving and from receiving it. You know, sadomasochism. That's probably worth talking about, don't you think? For instance, we might look at the question of why people find this option attractive, or what benefits it might confer upon its participants. We might want to discuss whether we ought to classify it as an aberration or an alternative lifestyle. And, I think it's important not only to hear about such things but to see an actual demonstration. Students learn in different ways, as you know, and some of you really benefit by having the visuals." Granted, a topic like this is probably better suited to a course in sociology, but my mind extended only this offer.

Mere intercourse with the Dean was one thing, but I wasn't convinced she'd help me illustrate sadomasochism. I myself knew nothing about the subculture, and didn't even really want to know, but a promise had been made and I'm a stickler for fulfilling vows. Plus, the cannibals just didn't pan out like I'd hoped. Something more would be required. (The cannibals, by the way, each were awarded with a $300 gift card to our student store. They were strongly encouraged to pick items that bore the school's logo, but most loaded up on candy, bug spray, sun screen, and small rotating fans, none of which were stamped with the school's logo.)

When I called the Dean to tell her about my hasty and imprudent vow, she surprised me by saying, "Sure, why wouldn't I help you?" She even offered to order a few items for the demonstration from a catalog that "somehow" had turned up in her mailbox but which she hadn't yet gotten around to recycling.

"It's got my name on it, Jack," she told me. "And I am the Dean, you know."

"Well, just pull the back page off and shred it," I said. "Then, you can recycle the rest." The Dean changed the subject at this point, but I was very happy to have her support.

On the day of our performance, attendance nearly matched what it was on the first day of class, and students seemed to be in a fabulous mood. Most were engaged in animated conversation, and I saw few electronic devices. It became clear to me then that the necessary steps had been taken.

The Dean arrived a couple minutes late dressed in a skimpy black leather outfit covered in pointy metal studs. She also wore a black mask with little bars over her teeth (similar to the one worn by Hannibal Lector) and unreasonably high-heeled shoes. Perhaps the best analogy I can offer is this: remove the studs and the bars from her mask, and she looked a lot like Cat Woman.

"Why aren't you dressed?" she whispered to me behind the podium.

"Well, I didn't realize that—"

"Ah, you're a lumberjack!" she said, clasping her hands together. "You'll be playing a lumberjack!" She was referring to my plaid flannel shirt, stone-washed jeans, and Bean snow boots, the get-up I had worn nearly every day since receiving tenure. The afternoon I was tenured, I packed up every tie, blazer, and starchy shirt I owned and dropped them at Goodwill for some other poor sucker. I am not exaggerating when I say that was probably the single happiest moment of my adult life.

"So, untuck and unbutton your shirt, will you?" she said, setting a small cardboard box on top of the podium. "And make it quick."

"OK." Apparently I was moving too slowly, because the Dean took over while I was still working the second button from its hole. Within just a few seconds, she had completed the whole row for me, exposing a very hairy Neanderthal-like chest that I'd never quite managed to own. "Arrrrgh!" I said.

"No, Jack, that's a pirate."

"Grrrrr," I said.

"You're not a bear."

"Then, what does a lumberjack say?"

"Not much. They grunt, I suppose. And they speak Swedish and Dutch and other difficult languages you don't know."

"There *are* American lumberjacks."

"Jack, why don't you open that box and pull out the whip. I'm going to jump in the swing." The prior evening, Jerry and I hung a swing from the ceiling. Neither of us had any idea what it was for, and neither of us really felt like talking about what it might be for.

"The Dean will know," Jerry said. I nodded in agreement.

The class grew quiet as the Dean clicked over to the swing and I began pulling the contents from the box: one whip still wrapped bound by twisty-ties, a pair of handcuffs, a rubbery strap-on dong of unreasonable length, and some kind of medieval flogging device. As I drew each item out, the class had a good laugh, which I was happy to see.

"Well," I said after emptying the box, "the day you've been waiting for is finally here. I trust that all of you will have the decency not to record what transpires this morning on your phones and upload it to the—"

"Professor Johnson!" cried Sarah. "The Dean's stuck! Help her! Help her!" I turned back, and the Dean was hanging from the swing by her foot, with her torso splayed on the ground in a most un-Deanly manner. Body parts that aren't normally seen on university administrative personnel could be seen. I jogged over to the swing and released her foot from her shoe.

"Oh, these damn heels!" she said. I helped her lay back on the floor. "Oh, Jack, I think I've really hurt myself."

"What do you mean?"

"I mean my back *really hurts.*"

"Can you get up?"

"I don't think so." I unfastened her mask. "Oh, Jack, the pain's spreading! It's like fire, it's like fire!"

"Sarah," I called out, "Call 911."

"Oh, yes, Professor Johnson! See, Professor Johnson, I knew this was a bad idea."

The Dean, it turned out, was nearly good as new after a few days of bed rest and a lot of pills. Fortunately, she had just strained a muscle in her lower back. The paramedics didn't even cart her away. Rather, I drove her to the clinic, and after an exam and a scan that turned up nothing serious ("I see a bulging disk," said the doctor, "but at your age, that's not anything to get excited about"), we went back to her place for dinner and had a good laugh. I asked her what she wanted me to do with the sex toys and the swing, and she just smiled. We really do have a hell of a Dean. I think we are very lucky.

I have learned that it is sometimes better just to stick to the script and not to worry too much about our best and brightest. Every generation has managed to figure it out, and I suppose this one will too. Plus, I've always liked the sound of a light rain. When all those heads are bowed, and all those thumbs are pecking away, I now imagine I'm sitting on my porch during one of those spring showers when the sun's still shinning, sipping sweet tea. Really, it's not half bad.

THE TUB

The two men knocked just as Roland had scooped his first spoonful of marsh mellow-encrusted yams. From between the blinds, he at first thought from their crisp white shirts and black ties that they were Mormons and cursed a little too loudly so that he felt he had no choice but to open the door. His yams, which he'd peeled and mashed and slathered in butter and sugar just an hour before, would grow cold now, and for this he was mildly resentful. He vowed then to scribble the letter he'd been meaning to send since having learned on PBS that the Church was trying to baptize just about every deceased member of the species by proxy. No one would make a Latter-Day Saint of his carcass, not now. He would make sure of that.

But the two men were not Latter-Day Saints or Jehovah's Witnesses or Gideons. (Do Gideons pester door-to-door? Roland couldn't recall.) Up close, they looked more like state troopers or FBI agents, or possibly Marines on holiday, dressed for the evening service.

Mr. Sims?

Yes.

I'm Agent Chrysostom and this is my partner, Agent Bavard.

Okay.

Well, sir, we've come to tell you that you've been chosen and that we'll be setting up a tub of water in your yard — out back or up front, it's up to you.

Roland was in no mood for whatever these hucksters were trying to pawn. His yams, which he'd slaved over and had cost him a hunk of skin from the tip of his finger, were getting cold.

I don't understand.

Even I don't understand, sir, as understanding isn't our business. But you've been chosen still, and we really should get to work before it all goes dark.

Work on what?

The tub, sir.

Jim Metzger

Roland glanced at Agent Bavard, mute thus far. He, like the other, had a mechanical, martial air and was riveted to the concrete upon which he stood, an obelisk of gravitas. The breeze, which fingered the mantle of foliage wrapped about the trees and bushes in his front yard, seemed to crook knowingly about the frozen pair. Their clothes flapped not a bit.

I can say more now, if you wish, or after. But bear in mind, the light is fading.

Now, please. Roland was in no mood.

We'll fill it for you, said the same one who had always spoken, and put a float in it – a ball, like in the old toilets. It's your job to keep the water level from going too low or too high, and the float will know when it does.

Roland wanted to slam the door on their stony faces and get back to life, but he heard his mother whisper something about manners – Now, Roland dear, how would *you* like to be treated? – and sensed that merely rotating a pine slab ninety degrees on its hinges wouldn't put an end to the matter anyhow.

The float will know? Roland wished to say Get the fuck off my porch just as Clint Eastwood might say Get the fuck off my porch, but he had said this instead.

Yes.

How?

A small chip – a microchip.

Oh. Roland scratched the back of his head, then his chest. And, if I don't maintain the water level?

You will feel pain.

How?

I don't know, sir.

You don't know?

I don't know. Roland wondered: Is it Halloween, or April Fools, or some other merry holiday I've forgotten? Long ago, when Roland had lots of friends and was buoyed by the endless possibilities that miraged before him, he might have had a little fun with the shenanigan, played happily along, thought nothing of the cooling yams.

What kind of pain?

They say it starts behind the eyes.

How?

I don't understand the mechanics of it, sir. That's for people above my pay grade to know.

So, what happens then? The one who had always spoken furrowed his brow. Actually furrowed his brow.

Understand, it's hearsay, what I tell you. I have no direct experience of it. But it goes down the spine, they say, like someone's screwing a vice around it, screwing down hard. Water gets too low or too high, they say it radiates to the extremities and lays you out flat, hurts like hell.

Then how can you be expected maintain the water level?

It's tough, I don't doubt that. But sir, the darkness is coming, and me and Agent Bavard got a little work to take care of, like I said. Right now I just need to know where you want it.

I don't.

But you've been chosen, sir.

Who *are* you?

Agent Chrysostom, sir, and this here's Agent Bavard.

Roland was beginning to wish that they had been Mormons or Jehovah's Witnesses or Gideons (if, in fact, Gideons do intrude door-to-door, although Roland was beginning to suspect they didn't go door-to-door at all but were the ones who shoved little green books in your gut right when you got off the bus and didn't yet have the wherewithal to motor left or right, avert your eyes, or muster a Go to hell – over which you would later agonize because you'd been brought up decently, but not quite so decently that you wouldn't mutter Go to hell when some stranger tried to save your soul.)

As Roland was thinking about the Gideons and their little green books, the agent who'd said not a word reached behind him, drew a pistol from his khakis, and shot Roland between the eyes.

When Roland came to, the crisp-shirted pair was bent over him, wiping blood from his forehead and dressing the wound.

What the hell are you–? Roland tried to ask, dizzy, still smarting from the tumble, the hole in his forehead.

Just relax, sir, said the one. It's nothing but a pin-prick. Pain should be gone by morning.

A pin-prick? You goddamn shot me in the–

A pin-prick, sir, I can assure you. Man up, will ya? It's really not that bad. Roland gingerly rubbed the side of his head, which had slammed hard against the concrete floor. A small knot was beginning to assert itself.

You guys are nuts! Get the hell off– Roland managed as the men struggled to hold him down.

The chip's lodged in your skull now. I recommend you monitor the tub. If you don't, you'll feel it. You'll see.

Roland tried to break free but found himself growing weaker, his eyelids drooping, his mouth going dry. Roland wasn't aware the mute one had rammed a needle into his thigh while he was out and injected an anesthetic.

I should also mention, sir, that it's in your best interest not to try to tamper with it – you know, cover it with something – a tarp, say, or a piece of plywood. The float knows when people tamper with it.

What the hell are you talking about? Roland slurred. Why would I tamper with it?

I just want to say good luck, sir. Know that you're not alone. There are others. They figure it out, they manage. You'll see.

What ... what others? Roland's eyelids had shut, and he was beginning to drool.

Just know that you're not alone, that's all. You're not the only one. And with that, Roland's brain surrendered to the serum. He went limp and his head rolled to one side.

The men carried him inside the house and laid him on his bed. Once they felt certain Roland's wound had quit bleeding, they strode silently out to their truck, loaded a large rectangular crate onto a dolly, and wheeled it to the backyard, where they set to work on assembling the cruel master that would ruin the sleeping man's life.

Roland didn't wake until late afternoon the next day. From the room's lone window, the creeping sun managed to engulf his entire body in its fire and raised his core so high that what woke him was the sweat that had pooled in his eye sockets and burned. The pain in his forehead wasn't gone as the men had promised, but it had subsided, or at least was less of a distraction than the rumbling in his gut and the aching knot behind his ear.

As Roland sat in the kitchen eating yams straight from the foil tray abandoned the day before, the newly installed tub caught his eye, its white porcelain gleam and cast iron clawed feet inviting closer inspection. Roland toted the tray outside, perambulated slowly about it, then peered inside, where a plastic sphere about the size of a softball floated above three or so feet of water. The waterline was between two thin black stripes that ran round the inside.

Kind of them to fill it, muttered Roland, as he thumped the ball with his middle finger and ran a hand along its cool smooth rim. The basin, plain but attractive, was antique – like something you might see touring an old country estate in New England, maybe. Like something fit for a Duke or a Queen. The men had set it high on a wooden platform.

Make a hell of a bird bath, he said as he walked back inside, foraging for a story he might tell his wife, who has due home within the hour from a trip upstate to her mother's.

We should call the police, said his wife, perturbed at her husband's recent misfortune, longing to plunge her tense frame into a warm candle-lit bath. The couple was standing quietly at the kitchen's bay window sipping decaf, working bits of vegetable matter from the interstices between their teeth.

Just let it go, Liz. They'd never believe me. Probably they'll lock me up for being such a goddamn loon.

What are you going to do with that thing?

Leave it for the birds. You like birds, don't you? Roland's wife massaged the back of her neck and quaffed the remaining ounce or so of black Columbian, bitter and tepid.

I do.

Although the couple didn't speak the rest of the evening, they did have a fairly successful go at intercourse. There was something about emerging from a bath naked and clean late at night, and there was something about warm soft skin, about a woman smelling so sweet. There was just something about it. So all the questions they might have had about this unusual event just vanished, as a chip of ice spit poolside under the noonday sun.

Jim Metzger

Not until the following evening did Roland begin to feel the first surge of pain – a new and unfamiliar kind of pain – between his eyes. Consumed with the tedium of evaluating stacks of student essays on their most memorable summer vacation ever, he had forgotten about the tub and the tiny hole in his head. At first believing the ache to be a routine occupational hazard no different from any other he'd gotten grading papers, he took a few ibuprofen and lay down. But when he woke at about 5 A.M., he noticed that it had worsened considerably and migrated to the base of his skull. It was no longer a mild ache that might be thrust from consciousness by focusing on something else but searing hot, impossible to ignore. He took three more ibuprofen and a couple of his wife's Pamprin, then reclined before the television, where he flipped aimlessly past local morning shows and cheery infomercials.

The flickering soon began to aggravate the tissues behind his eyes, so he stepped outside and watched kitchen lights snap on up and down the broad familiar avenue he'd called home since he and Liz had been married. A faint pink glow could already be seen through the tall pines that flanked one side of their property and soothed him. He thought of stalking hungry largemouth with his brother on mornings like these, of the implacable eerie misty calm of the ponds they frequented, of his line as it began to grow taut and move slowly on its own, and of the magnificent pleasure that once gave him. An open-topped Bronco rumbled slowly by, and the flannelled old man inside who delivered the paper heaved a package end over end that struck Roland on the crown of his head. A not quite genuine Sorry buddy could be heard from the cabin just as another package landed in his neighbor's driveway. Roland waved weakly then turned and bent to grab the morning news. The pain seemed to be getting worse and traveling down his spine. This seemed odd to him. Ibuprofen had never let him down so spectacularly before. He hadn't expected much from the Pamprin.

As he reached for the handle to the front door, the thought that probably should have occurred to him earlier finally did: maybe there was something to that tub after all. He jogged around to the backyard and peered inside the porcelain bath. The water level was flush with the bottom line.

There's just no damn way, he muttered to himself, glaring at the inert ball. Angry at himself for entertaining the possibility that a plastic ball could be responsible for the pain, Roland scooped it out and made as if he were going to hurl it into his neighbor's yard but fell to the ground and let out an agonizing cry of the sort one imagines when a man runs a finger through a band saw or when a soldier's leg is blown to tiny bits. Roland arched backward horribly too, as if he'd just had a thousand volts shot through his scalp to the base of his spine. And while fumbling violently for the dropped ball and cursing and biting his tongue and wriggling maniacally like some worm with its head mashed under a boy's shoe, he grabbed for a hunk of bark and rammed it sideways into his mouth, which didn't help with the pain as the movies suggested it might. The man screamed a ghastly scream and pounded at the wet grass and kicked and thrashed and bit his way toward the ball and having seized it somehow stood shaking and writhing and flailing while cussing in the most deeply offensive ways. When the ferocious thrashing thing bleeding now from its mouth dropped the sphere back into the tub, it fell limp in a livid heaving heap beside the wooden platform and moaned softly. When a woman came running out of the house in her bathrobe and squatted beside it crying and frantic and stroking its hair, it waved her away sharply and swore and curled up tightly into some kind of fetal position. As she yelled Honey! Honey! What happened to you? What's happened? What's happened? and turned back toward the house and ran, he stood and walked toward the spigot and cranked it once and dragged the hose to the porcelain bath and filled it til the water came up just a fraction below the top line. Still bleeding from his mouth and with the iron glare of someone to whom the gravest wrong had been done, to whom no greater wrong could be done, he lumbered toward the shed, fished around in the dark for caulk and a roll of screen he'd saved to patch holes so he and his wife could eat burgers and sweet corn on their porch in peace, harassed no longer by those rude bloodsuckers that seemed to have no other purpose than to make all of God's other creatures suffer, and quickly fixed a sheet to the top of the tub while cursing the gods above, evening naming the ones he could remember, so that the ball would stay where it must and he wouldn't be reduced to a mound of searing writhing flesh ever again. As he applied the caulk and bled and cursed, his wife ran panting and shaking out of the house with the phone in her hand and told him that an ambulance was on its way and that everything would soon be fine. She drew him close and questioned him ceaselessly about the events of that early morning, but he just applied caulk and pressed down on the screen and bled seething in silence, glaring and cursing like some possessed thing.

When the ambulance arrived, Roland fled upstairs and got in the shower. From the shower he yelled down at the paramedics and his wife and told them to leave him be, that he had things to do and would be fine, just as his wife had said. What he had to do was bleed a little more from his mouth and curse. After that was taken care of, he crawled under the covers a different man and fell asleep.

Hours later Roland woke cold and afraid. He slipped a sweatshirt over his head, finally knocking free the thin square of gauze the men had taped between his eyes, and stumbled downstairs to check the water level in the tub. He noticed that his wife was sitting at the kitchen table with her face in her hands and that his tongue felt huge and hard and sore. The slightest movement, the slightest tap against the inside of his teeth, sent a wave of hot pain through his whole face and neck that suggested to him he'd be taking his food puréed through a straw. He wanted to cuss at this discovery but couldn't.

He went back in the house and scribbled instructions on an envelope, then passed it to his wife. Once she had gotten hold of herself, she called the community college where her husband toiled for little money and told them he'd come down with a stomach virus and likely wouldn't be back in until next week. The kind woman of advanced age who'd picked up the phone said she wished him well and that she would lift up his name during a prayer meeting later that evening. His wife said that it was such a minor thing, really, and that the creator of the universe probably had more important matters to attend to. Naturally, the woman insisted.

For the next several days, Roland assiduously monitored the water level in his tub. Occasionally, he would scoop out just enough with a measuring cup to bring the water flush with the lower line, and each time he did, a dull ache formed between his eyes. And when he removed a smaller amount with a teaspoon so that the water dipped below the line, the ache spread suddenly and sharpened, reminding him of the moment he'd recklessly flung the sphere from its proper place and collapsed writhing on the ground. The very same thing happened when he added water so that the level was flush with the top line. And again, when a teaspoon or so was poured in so that the water inched just above the black line, pain migrated to his vertebrae and sharpened. All this time, while Roland experimented cautiously with the tub, testing to see exactly what kind of hold it had over him, his enormous sore tongue diminished slowly in size, which pleased him. But Roland was on edge.

Roland didn't return to work until the middle of the following week because he couldn't talk like a normal human being, and because he felt that talking was a critical part of his job. Some of the students who liked him a lot razzed him about his inability to clearly articulate about half his words and about the occasional bit of drool that would pool at one or the other corner of his mouth. Other students felt squeamish when he spoke and wished to be somewhere else.

The teacher gave the appearance of taking the whole affair in good stride, although on the inside he felt like a squirrel caught in traffic, fretting endlessly over the water level in the tub, imagining against his will all the one-in-a-million things that might cause the water to plummet or spike unexpectedly. When Roland's brain was underemployed, as it was, for instance, when he was in a staff meeting or brewing coffee or taking a leak, it would inconsiderately hurl the most implausible scenarios at him one after another.

By the end of the spring term, Roland's Chair, a stout fellow whom Roland felt enjoyed his power too much and probably hadn't had an original thought in a decade, began to get wind of the young teacher's more frequent comings and goings and noticed that his office door was nearly always closed now. The Chair questioned the employee about this one afternoon, wisely framing the discussion with the most sympathetic remarks about Roland's welfare. Their conversation, insisted the Chair, wasn't about job performance at all. Not yet anyway. Roland responded vaguely with copious hemming and hawing, in the end randomly pinning blame on a strained marital relationship. The Chair nodded thoughtfully, said he understood and hoped things would improve, and that if they didn't he knew a lovely young psychiatrist who could help get the couple back on track.

I do appreciate it, Bob, said Roland as they shook hands that afternoon, knowing full well that his habits weren't about to change, that in fact he was growing even more obsessed by the day, and that his relationship with his wife was, at the moment, the least of his worries. She would stick by him until he got this thing figured out, he thought. Some time ago she'd made a promise — for better or for worse, he seemed to remember her say.

Having been scared into adopting an obsessive-compulsive temperament foreign to his prior easy way, Roland managed to make it through the semester with few oversights or mishaps. There were times when he had to be away from the house all day and evening and the water would creep down a touch too far, triggering first an ache in his forehead and then the stabbing searing sensation in his upper vertebrae, but he always found a way to excuse himself and get home before going mad with pain. Heavy rains caught him off-guard several times; it was, in fact, the sudden downpours that terrified him most and sent him into a blind white-knuckled panic. Harrowing too were the heavy winds that swept down into the porcelain bowl and stirred things up beneath the float, sending seismic jolts of pain through his whole body that made him look like he was being stuck with a cattle prod or shot with a Taser. He tried constructing a barrier around the tub to stanch the wind, but the crisp-shirted men had been right: when the walls reached a height at which they might actually do some good, somehow the ball sensed interference, that the tub was being shielded artificially from the elements.

Summer, brutally hot in these regions and prone to the most outrageous thunderstorms, created even more trouble for Roland. The scorching midday sun seemed to suck water straight from the basin as if from a straw, as if it wanted to keep Roland on his toes, even to watch him suffer. Roland learned that he could remain away from the tub no more than four or five hours at a stretch, so he dashed home between sections (to help pay down student loans, Roland stupidly agreed to teach two remedial reading courses during both summer sessions) to refill the tub. During the most vicious thunderstorms, he simply excused himself from class and thrashed about in his office until it had passed, emerging later with cuts and bruises over his whole body. On a few occasions, the downpour managed to outpace Roland as he sped home so that he stood from his car raving mad, his back wickedly arched, blood from his tongue streaming down his chin. While he always somehow managed to scoop out enough water before losing consciousness, the incidents were beginning to take their toll. A man can only take so much abuse before the fragile structures of thought carefully constructed over a lifetime to give a little order to this place begin to crumble.

And crumble they did. Having been moored ruthlessly to the present, returned to that brute animality our species labored so hard to transcend, a mere responder to stimuli, nervous always, keyed-up, frightfully tense, Roland lost sight of the past, lost his taste for the future. He thought constantly about the tub, always and only about the tub. What few pleasant memories remained were overshadowed by those moments when Nature had outwitted his relentless vigilance and coerced from him a primal scream.

And so his mind became dominated by this singular obsession: he must do everything in his power to prevent the water level from surpassing either line. Everything else in the multiverse had ceased to matter.

After a difficult (some might say harrowing) summer, the harassed and tethered teacher began to lose control. He woke to find that he was not free, as the great French philosopher once had said. Pain, or the fear of it, had become such an imposing omnipresent specter in his mind that he saw or thought about little else. He had become a driven animal fitted with blinders, tugged this way and that, slashed from above, heeled from the side, commanded when to go, when to stop, when to lie down. He was a man no longer. And as he began to concoct ever more fanciful excuses for declining invitations to dinner or cocktails with friends, to barbeques and pick-up games after work, his social life so atrophied that the only conversations he ever had outside the college – and these, only of barest necessity – were with his wife. Not much could be said for their terse business-like exchanges. They went something like this:

Shall I pick up some milk, then? Roland might say at the beginning of a meal.

Sure, if you want, his wife may reply.

Can you do the dishes again? Roland may ask at the end of this same meal. My head hurts, and I've got to fill the tub. Then his wife would rise silently from her chair as Roland walked out the back door to address this most intractable issue.

It is true that their conversation was somewhat more involved the evening Roland informed his wife he'd been let go from the college.

What reasons did he give? asked his wife.

That I was late for class and didn't fulfill my office hours. And that I wasn't coming to staff meetings, or leaving them early.

Is that true?

Yes.

Will you fight it?

No.

His wife must have been irate when she heard this, but she showed no sign of it. She simply dropped her head and finished her meal. When she was done, she stood and spoke once more to her husband.

I will work more hours, then, she said.

The sacrificial gesture would have been duly noted by most men, but Roland was no man. He was beyond caring. She might have said, I'm leaving you, or, I love you, but neither declaration would have had any effect upon Roland, for he was no man. And he knew that all love was conditional anyhow, no matter what the preachers and the people in Hollywood had forever been telling everybody. She might love him today, he thought, but it couldn't last. You can't love fear and instinct, and that's all Roland really was. She still looked at him through their shared history, through all the wonderful memories they'd created together. But this was an error, and it perpetuated a wildly distorted of image of her husband that had nothing at all to do with the tethered and driven thing he had become.

I can't do this anymore, said his wife inevitably one evening that fall. The couple was again standing side by side before the kitchen window, sipping coffee, staring blankly at that porcelain fiend. Roland had just scooped about a quart of rainwater from it because his head hurt.

I'm not fond of the situation, replied Roland.

Roland hadn't given much thought to his wife in the past several months. She had become to him a kind of permanent fixture in the house, part of its furniture. He watched her as she perused glossy catalogues and thought about things they might buy for the house, or as she surfed the web for some hauntingly beautiful and secluded spot to which they might go to rekindle their love. Roland saw no point in either of these activities, so completely riveted he was to the two thin black lines that now defined his life. Sometimes his wife spoke of kids too, and Roland resented her deeply for this. Could she not see that he was no father? Fatherhood was for the tub-less, for those who still had leisure to give the future a look.

I want you back, she said.

Is there something left to want?

I want to believe there is. Her voice may have cracked, but Roland wasn't sure, and he'd fallen out of the habit of checking.

Why do you want me back? asked Roland.

Because I love you.

But her love wasn't enough. Roland suspected he might still love her too, but he couldn't coerce his gaze away from the tub long enough to test the theory. He had been driven mad, and he knew there was no coming back. He told her so one evening over dinner, and did it in an uncommonly cruel way to drive the point home, to drive her away.

I am ruined, he said. I cannot love you. I do not love you. It is time for one of us to go.

She took the hint – she was not stupid. She packed her things and moved to an altogether cooler climate, where she purchased a small home that had no tubs at all, only a shower. There she sadly began a new life without Roland. Soon she married and had babies and bought nice things from catalogues and took exotic vacations exactly twice each year, but never again was she truly happy, aware that such a thing as happened to Roland could happen. Most of the time she was fine because of the endless distractions of raising children and putting money in the bank, but if one looked closely, there was to be found a profound and irremediable sadness in her eyes, and she often wept late at night after her new husband had fallen off, perplexed and angry and numb that such a thing as happened to Roland could happen.

ROUND THE WHEEL

I didn't want to do it. But Dad kept giving me the look, like something a Tea Partier'd give a single mom on food stamps.

I was sleeping late, but so were all my friends. And it's not like I wasn't doing anything. Every day I was doing something, like fishing or playing ball or tossing the Frisbee. Like reading novels and the newspaper, and even thinking long and hard about what I'd read. Midsummer, I'd already plowed through a couple of Camus's novels, a little Hesse and Hemingway too, and God knows how many of those multipage features in *Newsweek* or *Time* or whatever was lying around the house. As I saw it, I was refining my intellect, honing my social skills, my coordination even – all things I'd probably need to please Dad down the road. It's not like I was smoking crack or nuking puppies or anything. Anyways, who was going to hire me for just a couple months?

"Oh, they'll hire you alright," he grunted one evening after work while sifting through a stack of mail. "And you'll learn a thing or two about what it takes to make a buck in this world. I guarantee you'll still have plenty of time to screw around with Jones and Turcott and all the rest."

Dad was a bootstraps guy, old-style, and still worked like a horse. Just vacuuming the house or washing the car, Dad was all in, grinding away with the steely determination of Rafa on clay, or Lance climbing the Pyrenees, soaking those ragged V-necks of his with the yellow pits and the collars that looked like they'd been yanked over the head of a steer. I admired him for this, although I was cut of different cloth, an alien and disappointing sort that hadn't turned up in our family til I was born.

So, because I didn't like the way Dad was eyeing me, all fierce and miffed-like, jealous, maybe, that I was having some fun, or worried that I'd turn out lazy and mar the family name, I peddled my bike down to the Piggly Wiggly and put in an application, which I hoped would be filed away and not looked at again until the store did a little spring cleaning, or went belly-up. With a name like Piggly Wiggly, I kinda figured that day wasn't too far off.

The manager called the house next morning at 8 A.M. sharp as my dad was suiting up for work. Mom didn't know exactly what to do with the call, being as I was still asleep, so she passed the receiver to Dad, who must said have something like, "Of course he'll be there!", because by lunchtime I was wearing a pink polo with a pig's head stitched over the nipple and watching some corny DVD about what made for proper manners. After a second DVD on hand-washing and packing groceries up right (eggs on top, put the Liquid Plummer in a different bag than the sweet corn, that sort of thing), I was led to lanes 11 & 12 and told to "load em up and wheel em out." "It ain't rocket science," the boss added as he slapped me a little too hard on the back. Well, that was the day I earned my first real taxed buck. I remember being so damn tired after that I didn't even feel like screwing around with Jones and Turcott and all the rest.

The polo chafed something fierce around the collar, and I didn't much care for wearing khakis in 98 degree heat, but the boss was decent overall and didn't ride us too hard. All summer long, though, it looked like I had scabies about the neck, but that was the only real suffering to come of the deal. I wasn't going to land some hot one anyway that summer, seeing I was still a gawky shy thing. Every now and then a plain-looking girl would say another plain-looking girl thought I was cute, but I couldn't find much motivation to act on that. It made me kind of happy for an hour or two, maybe, but that's about as far as it went.

I remember that sometimes a kid would blow chunks in one of the aisles, or a frazzled mother would drop a jar of pickles, or some granny's scooter would clip a display, sending the bulk of whatever we'd so diligently stacked tumbling down. Once, Lloyd, one of those old guys who'd made a career of it and still took the bus everywhere, found a monster tarantula in the bananas. Guess it hitched a ride all the way from Panama or wherever. After tossing different stuff at it to see what it would take to piss it off and make it bare those fangs, Lloyd heroically scooped it up with a shovel and dumped it in the mop bucket, where he drowned it by knocking it on its head every time it'd come up for air. That was quite an event, and it took up a whole half hour. We talked about it for a couple weeks, maybe, after. Lloyd was loving it, I mean really loving it.

There was Amanda, too, a cashier who to this day remains one of the hottest things I've ever seen. She was tall and tan with the sort of cleavage that makes you ache something awful inside. She had dark brown eyes, tattoos in just the right places, and an overall dangerous look that promised forbidden pleasures we peasants couldn't even dream of. That scabies-inducing pig polo (the women had to wear them too) could do nothing to mar her beauty. Although she lived in a double-wide with her stepfather and a mess of thin cats, we knew she was way out of our league, which kept things light. It's not like any of us got the idea of asking her out or anything; we knew our place in the grand scheme. Plus, she had this chopper-riding boyfriend, older, with lots of dark stubble and large unfriendly tattoos. Sometimes he would pick her up from work and stare hard at us while he waited, like we were the devil's spawn or something, or hell-bent on stealing his woman. I was so happy to see him go. But he didn't stop our eyes from feasting shamelessly on his girl when he wasn't there. Even the boss, a fat married guy with Jesus stickers plastered all over the back bumper of his Caravan, couldn't help himself. I'm sure she would have won bikini contests if he'd let her compete, but he wasn't that sort: he had to possess any woman that rode on the back of that bike.

I remember one time when it was just the two of us sitting on milk crates out back on the loading dock. She lit a cigarette, then offered me one. I'd never smoked before, but I said yes like it was no different than stick of Wrigley's or a Rollo. She went on about how she was going to get out of this place one day and get an education but that she had no money for luxuries like that, and couldn't bear to leave the fate of all those thin cats to her stepfather, who had no regard for any of God's creatures except himself. When I kept coughing, she turned to me finally and laughed, then slid her crate right up next to mine. She wrapped her arm around me, drew me close, put her hand on mine, shifted my fingers around so I didn't look like "a little girl holding a lollypop." My face had never been just a couple inches from a pair of that caliber (from any pair at all, really), and I nearly passed out from the sight of them, all mashed together and encroaching on me like that. She smelled like the inside of one of those high-priced candy stores at the mall, and her body was real firm, athlete-like, not soft as I'd imagined it.

Jim Metzger

She drew the cigarette to my mouth and told me to breathe in nice and slow, to hold it for a split second, then to let it go. I did like she said, as if she were some sage of vice or something, and it worked like a charm. My mouth felt kind of hot and stale, I told her afterward. She laughed and held me as I watched the pair jiggle and began to wonder more about them. She was so tender to me, so friendly and wise, so dangerous. I've felt that good once, maybe, in the ten years or so since. I must have been in heaven, as they say, as I can't imagine anything finer. But my imagination isn't anything to write home about.

We sat close, our shoulders and hips and knees sharing the warmth, as she talked about all she wanted to do in life, not once about that Harley-riding fiend. When our cigarettes burned down to little soggy ashy nubs, she stood and stretched and reached out a hand to help me up. Reluctantly I parted with my crate, with her, who had been to me for those few moments on the dock vixen, sage, and some kind of big sister all wrapped up in one. And, as if punishing me for having peered into paradise, the boss slapped a putty knife in my hand on the way back into the storage room and instructed me to chip fossilized bits of gum and muck from the tiles in frozen foods. I remained there on my hands and knees til closing, increasingly jaded for knowing there was some bit of heaven out there I couldn't ever have.

I was glad when summer was over and I was free again. The paychecks were so small, and didn't seem a fair exchange for all the vomit and pickle jars and wrecked displays I had to clean up, for all the rich ladies who looked right through you and barked orders like you were some mule, for all the bags I had to repack because some pursed-lipped beady-eyed thing from the Cretaceous hadn't been laid right in half a century, for all the ache I felt watching Amanda drag cans of soup and boxed waffles over that glass plate, for all the pity and terror I felt hanging with Lloyd, sensing all the while that it wouldn't be but a thing for me to end up a career grocerist at 50 too, that life was going to do whatever it was going to do without any regard at all for what I wanted. Man, I was glad when summer was over.

Later that fall, a buddy told me about a cash-paying job selling Christmas trees – right there in the Piggly Wiggly parking lot, as fate would have it. We had just gotten out on Christmas break, and having taken to screwing around and sleeping late the minute that final bell rang, Dad started giving me the look again when he'd get in from work, so I told my buddy, Let's do it.

There were two things I loved about the job: hulking sappy needle-y evergreens over your shoulder and tossing them on top of a car made you feel more of a man than you really were, and all the pretty girls were in such good spirits (because it was Christmas, of course) that you got the impression some of them might even be into you. It was an illusion buoyed by the cheer in the air; we knew that, but played along all the same, just like people do on Christmas morning when the preacher reads stories about traveling stars and virgins having babies and angels singing in the sky. I especially loved it when a rich lady all bundled up in fur would make you cut a tall one to just the right length, because then I got to swing the chain saw around and make some noise, and there's hardly anything in the world that makes you feel more of a man that chewing up wood with a chain saw. The cash passed out at the end of the night was pretty sweet too, far more satisfying than the sliver of a paystub from Piggly Wiggly that showed how much the government wanted for its battleships and fighter jets.

But the boss was a wild animal, disposed to fits of rage and the crudest sort of talk. He came down from Appalachia every year towing a camping trailer behind a red dualie. He lived right there in the parking lot for four whole weeks, tossing back tall bottles of the clear stuff one right after another, slurring orders to us kids from a little window in his trailer where he took the happy people's money, and always breaking some seriously foul wind, *Blazin' Saddles*-style. He was a wide grizzly fellow with dark teeth and a wandering gray eye, and he had a mess of coarse hair bursting from his stocking cap, from his undershirt, from his nose and ears even — a real beastly sort all around.

I remember one night, after the crowd had thinned out and we boys had begun picking up the twine and sweeping the needles into piles, he came crashing out of the trailer cursing my buddy's name, cradling a bottle of Everclear in one hand, waving a shotgun with the other. From what we could make out (he was slurring something fierce), it seemed he thought my buddy was pocketing cash payments for himself and then telling customers there was no need to make a trip to the window. But he wasn't. I worked alongside him pretty much all night long, and I've never known a worse liar. On the rare occasion he would try to pass some lie over on his buddies, he'd look away all of a sudden, get pretty white in the cheeks, and starting gnawing on his lower lip. He had no stomach for lying, and was maybe the most honest guy I've ever known.

The boss came right up to him and raised the shotgun to his forehead, cursing and splashing that grain alcohol every which way with his wild gesticulating. We all gathered round quick and started searching each other for some kind of cue. I couldn't find one, and neither could anyone else apparently, because we all just stood there dumb-faced, like it was the TV we were watching. My buddy kept insisting that he'd always sent folks straight to the window after he'd loaded up their trees, but that animal would have none of it. He cocked his gun and instructed him to turn out his pockets. My buddy did like he said, and nothing fell out but a set of keys and half a dog biscuit covered in lint.

"Ware'd ya put it, then?" he shouted as he jabbed my buddy in his crotch with the tip of his gun. "You hidin it down with your pecker, you crafty little bastard?" He kept on jabbing, but my buddy stood his ground with his hands raised up high, like he was being arrested. "Take em off, then, goddammit! Lemme see!" My buddy wasted no time dropping his drawers, but as he did one of the older grizzled locals who'd been working this lot for years came up behind him with a log and knocked him hard on the back of his noggin, which sent the boss face-first into a pile of shavings. As he hit the ground, his gun went off, and the bullet lodged in one of the tires on his trailer, which dropped loudly on its rim at an awkward angle.

The grizzled fellow got a bunch of us to help haul the boss back into the trailer, where we laid him on a bed littered with bent-back bottle caps and half-eaten bags of pork rinds. Above the panting of a fat naked pair on TV, one of us asked if he was going to be alright, bleeding a little behind the ear as he was, but the old local assured us that it "waren't nothin but a scratch" and that he'd be "good as new by sun-up." Because he wore one of those green Vietnam-era jackets and was pretty old, we took his word for it and began heading for the door. As we were knocking our way down the stairs, the grizzled fellow suggested we go ahead and pay ourselves from the register, seeing as we hadn't been paid yet. My buddy said he was just happy to be leaving with his scrotum in one piece and didn't want any more trouble. I told the man he could have both our shares. He was a real rough one and looked like he needed it more than we did.

My buddy and I never went back, but we were four days shy of Christmas anyhow. I was eager for it to be over. The novelty of feeling more like a man than usual and believing the lie that girls were into you was wearing off. I was tired of being cold all the time too. Plus, none of us really belonged there long-term anyway, or understood the Appalachian like the grizzled vet did. I suspect he went back, mainly because he had to. We all had daddies with spiffy office jobs who would give us a respectable Christmas and make sure we had plenty to eat. I thought that night about Lloyd and the vet, though, and it unsettled me some. I wondered too if the other boys at the lot ever had the same fear that stalked me – that maybe you'd wake up one day wearing a Vietnam jacket for real, or wearing a pink scabies-inducing polo for real, with your name tag pulling two little holes above your left nipple.

I told her I had no experience at all, but she hired me on the spot anyway. Was that even rational, in the best interest of the company? I think not. She immediately began inserting my name into these black rectangles on a whiteboard, and as she was, I began having second thoughts. I was thinking, Maybe just put me in for fifteen hours or so and let's give this a test run, but she was having different thoughts.

The job was actually pretty easy. Groups of people would sign up for one of the hotel's banquet halls, where they would hold conferences and share a meal or two, and we would set up the rooms the way they wanted, monitor the coffee and water and such during the meetings, and serve them food when the time came for that. I guess we were basically just waiters who did some heavy lifting before and after.

Most of the guys were athlete-types – confident, clean-cut, handsome. Not all the girls were into sports, but none were waifs either. There was only one ordinary little guy like me. He came from somewhere in the country and drove an old 280Z, which he was endlessly remodeling. Sometimes it showed up in the parking lot with no headlights or seats or bumpers. Once, it showed up stripped of all its paint and riding low on boat-trailer tires. He was quiet but always really cool to me. Whenever our conversations limped along, I'd just ask him about the 280Z and things would perk right up.

I liked all the athlete-types too, though, and they seemed to like me. But it's like they were a whole different species or something, and saw the world as one giant oyster for their taking. There were super positive about life, about the future, and seemed used to getting what they wanted, especially when it came to girls. And these guys weren't even football players; they were just track people and swimmers and golfers, but they had all the confidence of football players. I sometimes wondered what good I might need to do in this life to come back as one of them. Would I have to work in a leper colony or join a monastery or start a homeless shelter, or could I just help old ladies with the door, or with their groceries? I was hoping the latter would take care of it.

The woman who hired me and told us when to come in and what to do was a hot thing. She was older than all of us by about a decade, but she seemed a lot younger than that, and not much different in the head than we were. She had long blonde hair, a tight butt and firm calves, a pair of ocean blues and an overall I-can-show-you-a-thing-or-two sexy look to her. She talked all the time about parties and passing out. I remember that she used the word panties a good bit, which was a huge turn-on. I wished she hadn't told us about the parties she attended, or sprinkled her stories with that word as often as she did, because it kept me from focusing on the task at hand. I hadn't learned yet the art of working and having a little fun at the same time; the two, I felt, ought to be kept separate. Plus, even if I would have entertained the possibility of merging the two realms, sometimes I felt like my brain couldn't handle both at the same time. But the athlete-types had no trouble with this. In fact, not only were they cutting up and having a grand old time, generally they were far more efficient than I was.

The athlete-types would hit on our boss just about any time the work slowed, and she seemed not to mind it one little bit. She would tell us how some days she didn't feel like wearing panties, so she wouldn't, and how on days she did wear panties, she couldn't wait to pull them off when she got home. She said most days they'd come off right after her shoes (she wore skirts almost all the time), and that she'd leave them right there in the foyer, on the wooden floor. When she got to talking like this, the guys would get quiet for a spell, and begin working their lips and tongues as if they were thirsty. It was about the only time they'd just not say anything at all. Sometimes I felt like I was going to pass out.

Although it seemed she led a charmed life, when I was around her I occasionally felt the same pity and fear Lloyd and the grizzled vet aroused in me. The first time I felt this way was when we walked out to the parking lot together after work and she unlocked the door to a Geo. Rarely could I say that my ratty Caprice was better than anyone else's mode of transport, but in this case I definitely could. Her two-door hatchback, slate-blue with three missing hubcaps, a coat hanger for an antenna, and bright red tape where the brake and signal lights should have been, was the smallest thing on the road at the time, except, of course, anything in the motorcycle genre. The engine sounded not much different than a moped's, and when she puttered away through the empty lot toward the exit, she looked no more substantial than a bug that could be whacked into oblivion at any moment. As it buzzed and sputtered on up the ramp toward the interstate, I found myself saying a prayer for her safe passage home among all those speedy giants that whirred by. I thought for a moment of that poor hapless creature in Frogger, and how one wrong move meant a mighty unforgiving splat.

The second time occurred after we waiters broke down the tables and stacked the chairs too soon, midway through a seminar on how to become a millionaire by thirty. When the participants arrived back in the hotel after a tour of our historic district and a visit to the house that last year claimed the world's largest ball of paint, they found an empty ballroom with a solitary athlete-type vacuuming in the corner. She hadn't instructed us to break things down; for some reason, we just assumed that the speaker had said about all there was to say on hawking beauty products and sex toys. But the hotel manager came at her like a caged tiger and thrashed her mercilessly right in the middle of the hotel bar, and right in front of the majority of the banquet staff. She really took it for us.

At first I admired her, and thanked her deep down, but I pitied her later that evening when I found her alone at the end of the bar, slouched over the counter, turning a red-rimmed glass round and round in her hand. Her long blonde hair hung limp and stringy about her bowed head, as if she'd set it just so to conceal her face. When she glanced up at the bartender to signal for another, I caught a glimpse of her face in the mirror behind the tap, and it looked as though she'd been crying. Her mascara was badly smeared, her cheeks were hallow and drawn, her ordinarily impeccably ironed blouse was wrinkled and untucked – she was not at all the perky sexy thing that made us go quiet, made our mouths go dry. She said nothing to any of us for the rest of the night, and when she puttered away in her toy car, its gears grinding away, its engine hiccupping, its muffler exhaling the dark oily stuff, my stomach drew up in a knot and I started to cry.

I'm not entirely sure why I quit. Boredom, probably, or the weariness of having to listen again and again to the athlete-types razz and proposition our boss in the very same way they'd always done. I never stopped liking my small shy compatriot, but after a while I just couldn't coerce myself into planting questions about the endless renovations to his 280Z, so things went quiet between us. And as I watched our boss more carefully, I began to notice a deep and irremediable sadness in her eyes, in her posture and gait too, a sadness her beauty must have concealed from me during those first months on the job. I saw a woman who, while flitting around from one party to the next, nourishing an ego on crude alpha-male banter and lusty propositions that often went nowhere, was stuck, or chasing wind, or turning circles – a hamster spinning round her wheel. It wasn't long before her sadness crept right on over to me and, like some kind of virus, took up residence and made the whole world go blue.

You may be right in accusing me of projecting my own stuckness onto her. I would not contest the claim. But nothing ever changed in that banquet hall, and it was this inertness, I think, this over and over and over, that compelled me to hand over my name tag and try something different. She hugged and even kissed me that final evening (which I shall never forget), and when we pulled apart, she looked at me as if she knew I knew her secret, and as if she knew I was fated for the wheel too. How could I have known something like that then? Who believes from the very start that their life will be but an endless chasing of wind or turning of circles, a long lonely going nowhere?

Twenty minutes, he says. The old suit at orientation told us, Thirty minutes for lunch, plus fifteen in the morning and fifteen in the afternoon, but the boss is now engaged to the suit's daughter and knows he can say, Ten minutes, if he wants. Probably he will once they get hitched.

I usually just shut off the engine, pull a tuna sandwich and a Mountain Dew from the cooler behind the seat, and watch the office-types across the street file out to their cars all dazed and squinty-eyed. They always seem in such a hurry and never look my way, so I lean back, kick up my boots and watch, sucking in air not saturated with exhaust, and trying to hear things again, to get the thump and clamor of that diesel engine out of my damn skull. And I think, too, about what it'd be like to sit all day in a clean cool quiet room all day like those office people, poking away at keyboards, grabbing at telephones, punching buttons on copiers and fax machines and coffee makers, mashing staplers, scribbling on long yellow pads, then coming home feeling pretty much like you did in the morning, with no aches, no grit in your hair, no blisters on your hands. I wonder: How is it that I'm sitting on a backhoe eating fish from a can, wearing a scratchy orange vest and a hardhat, and the people across the street are sitting in the cool quiet, their brains not pummeled to mush, their ears taking in inoffensive sounds like doors clicking shut, like chairs scooting back, like co-workers asking, How was your weekend?

I tried college, I did. But those looks of Dad's would come at me sometimes, when I was reading a bit of poetry, for instance, or when I was trying to write some paper on how women get a raw deal in Hemingway. So my brain would tell me to get up off my ass and get a job, and I would, but that job would wear me slam out, eventually run me right out of school. I know what you'll say, and I'd probably say you're right in saying it. You'll say, Well, why the hell would you go and do a dumb thing like that? And I'd have no answer for you. I'd shrug, maybe.

I guess what I'm really trying to say is that I wished I'd kept on reading and thinking and not paid any goddamn attention to those looks Dad gave me. Don't get me wrong, I'm not blaming Dad for anything. I just wish I'd not let those looks do such a number on me, get stuck way down deep and let them toss me this way and that. Because once I'd gotten into the slaving way, I just stopped thinking like a college-type and never got back in the habit.

I'm paycheck to paycheck now, job to job. I'm Lloyd, that grizzled vet, that hot perky thing with the sad eyes. I sometimes wonder if they're still on the wheel, and I sometimes wonder what more I could have done to land a spiffy office job with a nameplate on the door, with my name etched on stiff little cards in my wallet, but that line of thinking's never turned up much. The hardest part's knowing you're just some expendable cog, some bit of machinery the boss can replace when it breaks or goes bad, knowing there's thousands of bodies just like yours out there that'll do just as well. Nobody ever tells you that you might end up just putting food in your mouth, putting in one application after another, putting one aching foot in front of the other. But they should. That way, when it happens, you're not so goddamn disappointed by it.

LARRY THE LETTER CARRIER

After possums had waddled up from the autumn scraggle and began dipping their snouts in the feed bowls of neighborhood cats and dogs; after raccoons had climbed from the storm drains and began pawing though cylinders of trash perched at awkward angles along the roadside; after good girls and boys had scrubbed their teeth and whispered short endearing prayers that made their parents smile; after Jon Stewart had elicited satisfying snickers from weary liberal suburbanites who at other times were just plain terrified of all the loony things the GOP might do; after children-ridden couples had given sex a feeble go and lay inert in a tangled heap of sheet and comforter; after sleepwalkers had secreted a few bites from some savory high-caloried treat and tumbled sated back into bed; and after the wrinkled old and chronic worriers everywhere had dozed open-mouthed and drooling before a poltergeist screen or those brightly colored bars, Larry the letter carrier fell from a high place onto concrete and knocked his skull so hard that he had not one more thought.

The sound, you may imagine, was a ghastly one: a single sharp crack – an illusion built of so many smaller cracks – accompanied by a colossal thud that for anyone looking on would have shook the tiny patch of Earth upon which she stood. But there was no one looking on. When the good citizens along Larry's route woke, they would think (if they thought about it at all) that as the young woman in blue stuffed their boxes with tightly wound magazines, windowed bills to darken their day, glossy ads for pizza and cheeseburgers and printer cartridges – well, they would think only that it must be Larry's day off. And when this same woman stuffed the day after, and the day after that, then for a whole week of days, they naturally would think that Larry had been transferred or promoted (for he really was a conscientious letter carrier), or maybe that he even had retired. After all, Larry was showing a little gray above his temples and through his enviably thick cenobite beard.

Now, following the event, the musings and twitterings from the few who knew Larry were predictable enough.

Thought two of his co-workers: *Poor guy. Must have been so lonely with no wife, no kids. Just can't imagine how dull and pointless it all was for him.*

Said the permed women who stood all day at the window passing out stamps and weighing boxes: "How anybody lets it get that bad, I don't know."

"Always a strange one, though. Like he wasn't there when he was there, you know?"

"But one of the nicest."

"He was."

"Such a shame."

"It is."

Said the boss with a grave and jilted look as he paced along the concrete lip of the loading dock: "I'll get someone in here quick as I can. Ain't no way I'm gonna leave the team in a lurch, trying to make up for what Larry done. The selfish bastard couldn't have waited til after the holidays?"

Said his very successful and very wealthy older brother: "Figures."

Said his ailing mother though a river of hot tears: "Now, what's he have to go and do a crazy thing like that for. Never thought of anyone but himself, that boy. Oh Larry, how can you do such a thing to your poor mother!"

Said the stocky plastic-smiled fellow who'd dunked Larry at twelve, reluctantly presided over his marriage to a garrulous Irish Catholic from Queens, and pleaded with him later on to get right with the Lord: "Pray for his soul is about all we can do, I'm afraid. Larry's gone and done a terrible thing." After finishing his pie, this same fellow set down his fork, quietly added: "But the Lord is merciful."

Said the grizzled bartender who passed pints of dark frothy beer weeknights to the bent-backed letter carrier and who spoke not a word unless spoken to: "It just don't work out for some."

All but the bartender got it wrong.

Now, let me tell you a little about Larry. Larry tried real hard. Sure, others have tried harder, but Larry was no slacker: A's, mostly, in high school; A's and B's in college (sometimes he drank too much, stayed up too late, thought about girls when he should have been reading the *Euthyphro* or calculating the area of a dodecahedron); A's, mostly, in graduate school, where he was working toward his Ph.D. until one morning in the lab he found all the white mice in his charge belly-up, their little mouths caked in foam and dark about the gums, like they'd been sipping hot tar or nibbling coal, which they hadn't. The mice belonged to his dissertation advisor, who – importantly – wanted to see whether listening to Britney Spears or to Brahms might enhance their ability to drop ping pong balls through rings for pellets of food. Naturally, the professor was angry when he heard the news, but he prided himself on being a rational man too, committed to the cool distance of the scientific gaze, so he told Larry over corndogs and tater tots the next day that he wouldn't hold it against him, that crates of fresh mice were already on their way and would arrive first thing Monday morning. But Larry knew that our rational part was no master – he was, after all, writing on Freud – and the professor, in spite of himself, couldn't help wondering what the boy had done wrong, or even if he had intentionally sabotaged the experiment. "Mice don't just up and die like that," his brain would tell him in the morning as he soaped and rinsed, bladed graying whiskers from his face, and munched through his Mini-Wheats. "But Larry's the most honest and conscientious student I've ever had," it would counter over lunch and through much of the afternoon. "Still," it would waver late in the evening, as the professor pulled the blankets snugly up to his chin and shut off the lamp.

And then there was the email, which Larry believed he'd sent only to the other graduate assistant who worked in the lab but had been copied to his advisor when he carelessly clicked "Reply All" while scavenging for a fry lodged between his crotch and the seat cushion. In the message, he had compared the sudden demise of the mice to the mass suicides of Jonestown and Heaven's Gate, commenting, "Guess the little guys couldn't hack old Haversham's obstacle course and those cheap-ass Walmart rock-pellets any longer and just opted out. Hell, I think I would have done the same thing if I had to work that damn hard for, like, Beanie Weenies or Spam or whatever. Hope they found the peace they were looking for, poor little dudes."

The remark might not have irked the professor had he been in a decent mood that morning, but he'd just learned that he'd been asked to teach two more sections of Introduction to Psychology because of the recent budget cuts and dropped his only remaining razor in the toilet, which left him with a very cold wet hand and some pretty gnarly stubble over just one side of his face. The Department, you see, had cut three term-faculty, which meant the tenured-folk would have to pick up the slack until people quit believing that tax cuts for the rich would magically benefit those who weren't and the Democrats won back the legislature. Old Haversham could be a cool guy, but he was in no mood that morning, and very few mornings after that. It seemed the free and easy exchange between professor and student had vanished overnight (those damned mice!), and without a sterling recommendation letter from his advisor, Larry knew he would have no shot at a teaching job. Six years of grinding labor and playing the sycophant had all come to nothing with the click of a mouse. Larry was just smart enough to see this, so he quit.

Larry couldn't quite see himself as a company man and recoiled at the thought of taking orders from intellectual inferiors, so over the next few years he tried his hand at a number of entrepreneurial ventures. For instance, with a small inheritance left by his grandmother he bought three acres of land and an old Winnebago and raised alpacas for a season, hoping to profit from their wool. But just weeks after their first sheering, the alpacas acquired a fatal intestinal illness from mushrooms that sprang up after heavy rains and passed. Nearly broke, the former grad student decided to use what few resources remained – an outdated computer, stacks of copiously footnoted hardbacks in psychology, and a brain that still functioned reasonably well a few hours every morning – to churn out a self-help book. The genre was red hot, he thought; the plan couldn't fail.

But it did. "Too much academic jargon," commented a soccer mom from Nebraska. "Reads like a dissertation," remarked a software salesman from Wichita. "Not vrey helpfull for improoving happiness felings," wrote a student from Phoenix. And they were right. But the book still managed to sell nearly two thousand copies during its first year in print, which left him with a whopping $1,850 in royalties, before taxes. Figuring in labor and home-office supplies, Larry calculated his pay to be somewhere in the neighborhood of 13 cents an hour and at that very moment decided not to become a writer.

Larry eventually stumbled into a tolerable job at the local newspaper where he met a reasonably attractive woman who occasionally made him smile and taught him to bake Bundt cakes. The two were aware they were getting on in years, and since the sex was just about what both expected, they wed, bought a fixer-upper on the wrong side of the tracks, fixed it up, and filled it with three adorable screaming kids.

Larry worked nights at the paper copy-editing for the Sports and Life pages, so he was responsible for picking up their eldest son Matt from school. One brilliant blue afternoon at pick-up, as Larry watched his son and several of his friends muff the soccer ball around on the playground, he found himself standing next to the mother of Matt's best friend. The two struck up a thoughtless conversation that seemed to be going nowhere until the mother was hit above the eye by an errant Frisbee, which drew blood. Larry was concerned, so he called out to Matt and his friend, informing them that he would be taking Ms. B inside for some First-Aid. The boys, maximally absorbed in the contest, could not have cared less, and likely did not even notice their parents' departure.

The vice principal pointed the pair in the direction of the nurse's office. When they arrived, they found the room dark but unlocked, so they went in and began rummaging for gauze, tape, and some alcohol. Not much was said. Larry cleaned the wound in a mindless perfunctory way as the mother sat erect and grimacing on the crinkly-paper. When Larry rubbed some alcohol on the gash, the mother squealed in an endearing manner and reached out for him, pulling him close. Larry noticed then that her hair smelled sweet, of lavender and coconuts, he thought, and that her breasts were warm and firm, which reminded him of turning tight circles with shy sweaty girls in disco-balled school gymnasiums. He sensed too that she was all alone in this big world, although he in fact knew not a single thing about her — whether she was married, for instance, or whether she had any kids other than the boy outside, or even her first name. "Ms. B," his eldest had always called her.

As Larry reached around to stroke her sweet-smelling hair, Ms. B peeled her legs from the crinkly paper, stood, and gently backed the well-intentioned responsible father of three against the wall. Heart rates rose, breathing grew shallow, eyelids began to fall, and rational parts suddenly ceded to animal parts, so that the two got irreparably tangled up until what had to happen happened. When it was over, Larry finished dressing the woman's wound with trembling hands as she straightened her hair and wiped sweat from her neck and brow.

Larry thought about the event a lot over the next several days and tried to figure out what had gone wrong. He recalled being in an unusually fine mood that day on the way to school, and having taken special notice of a large green tractor as it clawed deep troughs into the dark steamy earth, and of a man wrestling a jackhammer into groves along the pavement. He felt that maybe these unfortunate sights had wakened something in him that spring day, that none of this ever would have happened had that careless kid thrown the Frisbee straight, had Ms. B not smelled sweet and given the air of someone not quite at home in the world, had she presented slightly saggier boobs more appropriate to her age. Most unfortunate of all was that Larry's strict upbringing had created an overly scrupulous conscience, which pressed him hard to come clean to his wife. This he ill-advisedly did late one night in the sack, post-orgasm, persuaded then that the strength of their marital bond might withstand any assault.

She was not pleased to hear it. In fact, she became quite angry, grew angrier by the day, stewing for pointlessly long stretches on the affair, thought Larry, who held an unfortunate concatenation of events responsible rather than himself. "As if there really is some unchanging, essential self we might blame," he added smartly the evening of the revelation. Larry's wife was put off not so much by the act itself but by his defense of it, and after stepping on an upturned Lego early one gray morning, she told Larry, who was dutifully packing up peanut-butter sandwiches and grapes and Oreos for the kids' lunches, to get the hell out and never come back. Well, that's just what Larry did, not because he wanted to, but because his wife had become a wild animal in the intervening weeks whom he no longer recognized and who began to scare him in ways he hadn't known since bullies first rose up in school and began to terrorize the well-behaved with great shouts and insults as they fast-fretted home. Larry felt both that his wife had every reason to go berserk and that he was somehow innocent, both that he was a felon and that things merely had gone wrong that blue day. But that's how Larry lost his wife and kids.

About a year later, the lonely and vulnerable man joined a conservative church much like the one in which he himself was compelled to make the good confession, curious to see if he still might be capable of the warm feelings he took comfort from as an awkward gentle lad, curious to see if he might meet a few young untroubled women there not yet ruined by life, but also because it was a mere two blocks from his miserable little apartment and held pig pickings every spring and fall that doused the neighborhood in the most sublime primal aromas. Larry didn't think much about what the scrubbed and smiling church folk actually believed – to tell the truth, a lot of it seemed just plain silly to Larry, although he couldn't yet articulate why – because there were several reasonably attractive women who sat up front and whose big brown eyes and big round breasts most of the time captivated his attention. They sat erect and earnest, brimming with hope and all things decent, he thought, lit up on the inside by something pure and true, yet still seemed in possession of all the animality that no religion, no zealous prophet of the Most High, could ever stamp out.

One afternoon, the pastor of this church, a small exclamatory fellow with a wide smooth brow and apocalyptic eyes, asked Larry to accompany him on visits to the elderly ill. About mid-way through each visit, whether asked or not, the little man would offer a lusty word-clogged prayer, then draw a jar of ointment from his hip-pocket. Having rubbed the goo vigorously between his fingers, the little man would quickly apply the sign of the cross to whichever body part had been ailing their host. Without fail, once the ointment touched the skin, the host would cry out how near she suddenly felt to God, how sure she was the Spirit had touched her, how she now knew that God would finally heal her. Often, they would bawl afterward too, which made Larry so uneasy that his skin became hot and prickly and he knew not what to do with his hands. Larry had been assigned no role in the drama and felt useless, so he went along only that one time.

Now, on the way back to the church that evening, the pastor pulled over at a convenience store for a Yoo-hoo and some Fig Newtons. While he was inside, Larry began rummaging for a napkin or two to wipe down his face and the back of his neck. When none could be found, he opened the glove box and there discovered something that surprised him: tubes of His & Her KY Jelly, each half-squeezed, rolled up from the bottom. Larry wasn't the sharpest tool but neither was he the dullest, so his mind managed to piece things together rather quickly, and as it did something deep within him recoiled at the notion that the Spirit might be purchased for a mere $11.95 at Walgreens.

When the two arrived at the church's parking bay, Larry mustered the courage to confront God's herald. The conversation went poorly. In the end, the pastor said he didn't care much for Larry's skepticism or his tone and thought it best that from now on he seek his spiritual food elsewhere. Larry would miss the full-breasted women who sat up front earnest and erect, but he took comfort that the biannual aroma of seared swine would still be his to enjoy.

The unfortunate event left Larry a bit jaded and raised questions for him, questions that before he never thought worth pursuing. After all, Larry was an American, and Americans assuredly believed in the Almighty and his watchful care over all God's creatures. The first question he asked, "Might it *all*, then, be a sham?," was too big to manage right off, so he thought of some smaller ones like, "If I'd been born in India, wouldn't I probably have been raised a Hindu and thought my whole life that Hinduism was the most sensible and natural thing in the whole wide world?," or "Can God really punish us for eternity for not being able to figure out which religion's got it right?," or "If God is God, why can't he find a way to make his will plain to everybody?" He'd heard these questions before, so he started with them, thinking deeply about them for the very first time, ashamed that he hadn't gotten around to it sooner. These questions led to even more like, "Would a good God really make a mosquito?," then, "What might we do to a fellow who created something like a mosquito and sent it into all the world to harass and slay millions?," which led to the purchase of a stack of books on the problem of evil, that intractable and damning conundrum that very soon foreclosed for Larry the possibility of believing in any kind of Creator concerned with our welfare.

Things might have been just fine had he simply quit being a Christian and turned to roller-blading or to noodling or to fantasy football, but for some reason Larry kept right on reading, eventually getting hooked on really bleak stuff by Lucretius, Schopenhauer, and Camus that convinced him the universe cares not a lick for us, that anything we do will come to nothing, that the world's sufferings far outweigh its joys, and that the dead are the most fortunate of all. The overall effect of his studies was to banish from him all fear of death, even to implant within him a mild desire for its arrival.

Now, Larry might just as well have read all kinds of literature that celebrated life – gather ye rosebuds stuff – but he didn't. Some take up a carpe diem creed when waking to the truth of a godless universe, but others just grow melancholy, and Larry found himself among the latter. I can't tell you why. Some kind of unresolved childhood trauma, maybe – your guess is as good as mine. I bet even Larry couldn't have told us why.

It was about this time that Larry became a letter carrier. He hadn't set his mind to it. Rather, a shy helium-voiced youth who worked evenings with Larry at the paper told him about an announcement he'd seen on a bulletin board when downtown contesting a fine for publication urination. (The boy was fishing, and a forest ranger searching the area for marijuana groves happened by just as he was zipping his trousers. There was nothing at all antisocial or perverse about the exposure of his privates to fresh air; it was simply a wrong-place/wrong-time sort of thing. In the end, the charges were dismissed.) The announcement said the government would be hiring three postal workers over the summer and promised "solid pay and respectable benefits." The youth said he enjoyed being outdoors and might have applied himself if it weren't for his ailing mother, whom he cared for during the day. Larry had never had "solid pay" or "respectable benefits" and happened to be in a bit of a funk at work, so he applied, took the civil service exam, and was hired on the spot. Later, he was told that only four people were interviewed, and one of these, whose hair seemed to lack order and whose clothes seemed more rumpled than they ought to have been for a job interview, gave some on the committee the impression of "mental instability." Among Larry's reasons for leaving the paper and striding about town with a large white bag was that thinking had never really gotten him anywhere. Sometimes it even seemed to make matters worse. At the time, he was of the opinion that the daily repetition of sorting and stuffing and scooting one's feet along the pavement might put his mind to sleep, which would enable him to see things more like otters and beetles. As it turned out, Larry was right, and life became more pleasant overall as a result.

The evening Larry knocked his skull on the concrete so hard that he had not one more thought was much like any other. He wasn't distressed or angst-ridden or angry or out of his mind. He was a touch melancholy, but he had grown accustomed to the feeling over the years, and had even acquired a certain fondness for it. It was, in fact, a desire to deepen a pleasantly somber and reflective mood that inspired him to grab a few beers from the fridge and climb the fire escape alongside the four-story brick building where he received his bins of mail to a small steel plat-form that overlooked the city. He had been there many times before and found solace in the spectacle of it all – the passing clouds, the mangy strays stealing from dumpster to dumpster, the lone pedestrians shuffling along hands-in-pockets, the rhythmic yellow flicker of the traffic lights, the wind's rousing of dry foliage and debris, the steam ascending from manholes and storm drains. How he hated to leave! For these moments nourished him like nothing else, and this night was no different. Cross-legged, Larry absorbed the subtle sensations of night, thinking little, sipping slowly, running his free hand methodically through that massive tangle of beard.

Until a small bug maneuvering along the edge of the platform caught his eye and he leaned over to see what it was. It appeared to him to be a ladybug. Having a certain fondness for ladybugs, he reached out for it, and lowered his index finger that it might climb aboard, but it turned back. Larry set down his bottle of beer, leaned in farther, and cupped both hands around it. And as he waited for it to ascend one hand or the other, he glanced out beyond the ledge, then straight down, fixing his eyes on the sidewalk below, which suddenly seemed so far away, and startled him. A dizzying panic overcame him, and his brain elected – oddly, maybe – to present for consideration the recent insight that the dead are the most fortunate of all. It might have sent along something else, like an image of his estranged children or his loving mother, or nothing at all, but it offered precisely this message, and only this message. Larry felt himself tumbling forward – over his hands, then over the ledge – and at some point became aware that he might prevent his going over, but the sudden calm awakened by the insight so pacified him that he just smiled and went limp. So over he went – not planning to, not wishing to, but not regretting it either.

Everyone but the old bartender will keep saying the event made per-fect sense because Larry had no wife and kids around, no close friends or hobbies they knew of, and appeared to be drowning his sorrows with booze when he hurled himself from a high place.

But it's just that a man saw a bug and had a thought.

THE
CONFERENCE

The robust rectangular edifice, once a tobacco warehouse, was layered in thin corrugated tin of the sort one often finds on old farms. Displayed just above the front entrance were massive red letters that boldly announced the church's name – Calvary United Methodist Church – as well as the denomination's logo, a cross enveloped by a flame to represent the descent of the Spirit at Pentecost. Pastors, mostly overweight balding white men in their 50s and 60s, were trickling in one or two at a time, several coughing fitfully while waving away particles of fine white dust stirred up by the flurry of Buicks, Crown Vics, and Chevy and Ford pick-ups that bumped mercilessly along the uneven, unbounded gravel parking lot.

Immediately inside was a foyer conjoined to two spacious hallways, both portholing to classrooms and restrooms. The sanctuary, where the main event would soon begin, was directly behind the welcome table, but the double-doors were closed, shrouded in a white sheet hastily inscribed with a large black arrow directing all traffic down the left-hand corridor to the cafeteria, where a great Southern feast was set to commence in a few moments.

Not yet recognizing anyone I knew, I filed mechanically down the hallway with the rest, scanning glossy advertisements for devotional literature and upcoming events, as well as a perplexing array of tacky Christian art gathered from attics and church basements: Anglo-Jesus posing with a group of toddlers in 50s attire; Anglo-Jesus holding a shepherd's crook and smiling lovingly; Anglo-Jesus standing tall in the middle of a Dakota prairie proclaiming good news to all, including a Disney-like mélange of cute furry critters and garden variety birds.

The cafeteria was nearly filled to capacity and vibrating with the cadences of spirited ministerial voices exchanging hearty greetings, inflected with anticipation for the great banquet. I took a seat at one of the secluded tables near the coat rack. A district superintendent in a dark blue suit strode to the standing microphone at the front of the cafeteria.

"Welcome!" he boomed. The cacophony gradually subsided, and a smattering of responses rang-out.

"Good morning!" said one.

"Good afternoon!" cried another.

"Great to see you, Hank!" bawled someone behind me.

"We've got an important task ahead of us this afternoon that will require our utmost attention," the superintendent began with stagy gravitas, "so let us nourish these bodies. Please give our kitchen staff here at Calvary a hand for the marvelous job they've done in preparing this meal. It smells delicious, doesn't it?"

"Hear, hear!" someone chimed, as we all applauded raucously.

"Before we dig in, let's thank the Lord for his many blessings." During the brief lull, while the superintendent was gathering his thoughts and wiping perspiration from his brow, someone at the end of my table knocked over his sweet tea and took the Lord's name in vain. Tea rivered to the tile below. Across the room, a cell phone feebly crooned "When the Devil Goes Down to Georgia" while the wait staff whispered.

"Gracious and most merciful heavenly Father," he began, "we gather here today in gratitude for all you have given us: sunshine, the company of good friends, a safe arrival, and good food. Bless this time together, that our conversation may be for the up-building of your glorious church. Let us cherish this brief time with our colleagues all across eastern North Carolina as an opportunity to rekindle friendships and reinvigorate our commitment to you, and to the truth of the gospel of your Son, Jesus. Guide our thoughts and words these next few hours as we ponder a tough issue, one that threatens to divide your sheep one from the other. Let us remember that you have encouraged us through your apostle Paul to be of one mind and put aside all fractious behavior, all useless quarrels, all fruitless controversies that undermine the unifying work of your Spirit. Strengthen us, holy and merciful Father, to defend the eternal and unchanging gospel, a light of truth to all the world against all ungodliness. Finally, we thank you, Father, for this bountiful meal; may it nourish and sustain us throughout this day and provide for a safe, secure passage back to our congregations and loved ones. It is in your Son's name that we pray. Amen."

Thank you Jesus! The feast had already been spread before us: no lines, no waiting, no difficult choices. At "Amen," we buried our heads and began devouring our BBQ chicken and sides lasciviously. At the end of my table, which appeared to have attracted a motley crew yet unacquainted with one other, a skinny guy with avant-garde spectacles and an earnest demeanor was trying to be friendly by starting a conversation. Apparently new to these parts, he didn't know that nobody gives a damn about that sort of thing at feeding time. The poor sap continued planting questions while we pulled and sucked, slurped and belched. What a sweet melody it was: the incessant drone of industrial rotating fans positioned in each corner of the cafeteria; the faint, undecipherable mutterings between bites; the squeak and squeal of greasy fingers and plastic forks on Styrofoam dinnerware; and valorous, carnivorous grunts. Occasionally, someone would rise for air just long enough to pass a side of mashed potatoes or baked beans, and it would run round the table at warp speed, returning to its point of origin wiped-clean. It was hard to imagine there were so many among us who actually believed we hadn't descended from slime and chimps.

After about twenty minutes or so, one by one we pushed back from the trough, loosened our belts, belly-slapped, back-slapped, and choired our hallelujahs. Drunk on chicken fat, gravy, and starch, we were like satiated men after the hunt, though we hadn't slain, roasted, or carved: we were served by black women dressed in white.

At about a quarter to one, we began shuffling reluctantly in the direction of the sanctuary, lugging swollen bellies sloshing with sweet tea. The sanctuary, an unadorned perfect cube, filled slowly. On a rickety plywood stage were a podium emblazoned with the UMC logo, flanked behind by U.S. and N.C. flags; a row of padded grey folding chairs for the panelists; a drum set tucked away in the back right-hand corner; and a mobile altar outfitted with six grocery cart wheels. As had become customary during these denominational gatherings, I chose a seat at the end of a row and pulled out a novel of no literary merit.

Promptly at one, the bishop, a stately boulder of a man who carried most of his four hundred-plus pounds between his chest and knees, ascended the stage, trailed by a modest entourage of district superintendents and other lower-ranking dignitaries. The panelists had already taken their seats and were talking casually among themselves. The bishop sidled

55

up behind the podium, flattened a few pieces of wrinkled paper with his palms, and took a sip of water. Then, at the bishop's gentle urging, the crowd began to grow quiet. He waited a few moments, glanced back at the row of panelists and luminaries, and spoke – as always – with great deliberation and ministerial affectation.

"It is so good to see you all again, my friends," he drawled, arms outstretched. "I so rarely see many of you, and it is so very good to chat and catch up. It is hot, our panelists are ready, and you all have sermons to finish, so let us turn to today's business without further delay." The bishop threw back his head and quaffed the remaining water with a single gulp as if he were downing a shot of tequila. Then, he dabbed his brow with a purple kerchief.

I knew little about the bishop. Two unremarkable memories come to mind. I recall that in one of his speeches he boasted disingenuously of having completed his "doctoral" work at Princeton. The bishop actually earned a Doctor of Ministry at Princeton Theological Seminary, a training school for ministers that happens to be located adjacent the University's campus. From what I understand, the Doctor of Ministry can be completed at one's convenience over a few summers and is much different from the Ph.D., which typically requires six to ten years of full-time labor. His attempt to pass off a Doctor of Ministry from a theological school as "doctoral work" from a prestigious university, which many ministers in the South routinely do (often successfully), was unflatteringly pretentious. I retain nothing else from this particular speech.

My other memory derives from a walk-a-thon sponsored by the United Methodist Church to raise money for diabetics in eastern North Carolina who either didn't have insurance or whose insurance did not adequately cover the cost of their medications. At the end of the event, trophies were awarded to people who had come in first, second, and third place by gender and age-group. I had walked the course at a leisurely pace with a group of people from my own congregation, unaware at the time that rewards for haste were to be presented at the event's completion. In fact, our group was among the very last to arrive at the finish line, where we found several participants perturbed at our nonchalance, itching to break into the leaning tower of warm Pizza Hut boxes.

After the meal, the bishop awarded the trophies, at which point I learned that I had managed to capture first place among males 25-35 years of age. The only reasonable explanation for my "victory" is that I was the only male participant in that bracket. The bishop, I believe, was aware of this fact, and when the time came for me to accept the prize, he handed it over with some embarrassment. We shook hands but did not exchange words. Oddly, I also remember that he was wearing fulgent orange Bermuda shorts and bright yellow Disney sunglasses with a Tweetie Bird logo affixed to its bridge. They detracted from the dignified aura that he more successfully cultivated in black robe and stole.

The bishop continued: "As you know, this issue has plagued our denomination and others for some time now. In fact, it threatens to divide some communions. We are not at that point yet, thank God, but we do need to have a frank, open conversation. We need to hear from people on either side of the issue. Homosexuality is here to stay, friends, for better or for worse, and we must address this with candor, and in love. I have articulated my position on the issue before. You all know where I stand. You know also where our denomination stands. As people committed to the authority of Holy Scripture, we simply cannot condone homosexual behavior, and we cannot ordain homosexuals into the ministry of Jesus Christ, as some are attempting to do in conferences around the nation." A few at the back applauded. One whooped. "Let me read two statements from the *Book of Discipline* as a reminder to you all." The bishop retrieved a pair of tortoise-shell bifocals from beneath the podium, gingerly fitted them about his temples, and pressed down once again upon the wrinkled sheet: "'The United Methodist Church does not condone the practice of homosexuality and considers this practice incompatible with Christian teaching.'" The bishop paused and ran his index finger down the page. "Hear also this: 'Although all persons are sexual beings whether or not they are married, sexual relations are affirmed only within the covenant of monogamous, heterosexual marriage.'"

The bishop pried the spectacles from his ears and stuffed them in some secret chamber beneath his robe. "There is, my friends, little wiggle-room here. The Bible and our tradition are clear. But it's high time clergy and laity in our Conference had an honest, respectful discussion about this issue. We are here to learn, to grow, to understand a little more deeply. We are here to listen to one another. Use this experience as a catalyst to get conversations going in your own churches, just as we all committed to do at our last General Conference. But always do so, of course, with the denomination's official stance in mind, and with the Holy Bible firmly in hand. *Always.*"

The bishop coughed and grabbed for his glass, now empty. One of his aids sprinted off stage in search of the wait staff. He wiped the perspiration from his brow and temples and continued: "I want to begin by introducing our panelists, who have so graciously agreed to be here with us this afternoon. To our far left we have Angela Howell and her parents Robert and Evelyn, who are from Farmville. Angela is a lesbian and revealed her – or, rather, 'came out,' as they say, to her parents in her sophomore year of high school. She is now in graduate school at ECU in English literature and lives with her partner Sandy, who, I understand, is in medical school, a Pirate as well. Did I get it all right, Angela?" Angela was conversing quietly with her mother behind Robert's back and hadn't heard the bishop. "Well, I guess that means everything's okay!" Many laughed, several heartily.

"In the center we have Todd, his brother Jack, as well as his mother Georgia, all from Morehead City. Todd, who 'came out' to his family after college, now runs his own business, an internet affair selling ... well, odds and ends, unique and interesting knick-knacks, one might say, for the homosexuals, for the gay people. His mother Georgia is an active member of Trinity in Morehead City and has been very open about her struggle to accept Todd's lifestyle. Thank you all for coming, and for your willingness to journey so far westward on a brilliant Saturday afternoon." The family acknowledged the bishop's gratitude with forced smiles.

"Last but not least, we have Tim and his partner Zack, both from Lizard Lick. Tim and Zack met in a high school theater class, it says here, and graduated from Pitt Community College, right here in Greenville. Together they own and manage a day spa downtown. Tim, I should say, explored a call to the ministry while taking classes at Pitt, which is how we got to know him. After a summer internship at St. James, Tim decided to move in a different direction, confident that God would use his gifts in other ways. We welcome both of you." Tim and Zack, the only panelists whose appearance might have suggested ties to the gay community, nodded affably. Both were in their late 30s, and their matching muscle T's revealed exceptionally tanned, chiseled physiques. "Tim and Zack are also married, I failed to say," added the bishop with a cough. "By the state of Massachusetts? Is that correct? Or, is it Iowa?" Clasping hands beneath the table, the couple nodded again, to which of the bishop's options it wasn't clear. "A warm, hearty Southern welcome to all of you!" the bishop exclaimed, generating feeble, uncertain applause. The bishop then introduced the moderator, a district superintendent about whom I knew nothing, and turned the remainder of the session over to him.

The moderator asked each of the gay panelists to talk about their experiences in the church, particularly as adolescents and young adults, and the circumstances that led them to disclose their sexual identity to their family and friends. All were uncommonly articulate: it was clear that they had been asked to speak publicly about the issue before.

Two aspects of their stories left a deep impression upon me. First, all spoke not as if this were a matter of the intellect or the will, like some acquired habit (biting one's nails, for instance) that they one day might decide to drop. Their sexual identity was part and parcel of who they had always been, and who they always would be. Being gay was like having brown eyes or broad shoulders, said Tim: it just *was*. They felt that God had created them this way, and that diversity in sexual orientation was woven into the very fabric of things when God fashioned the world, part of what God saw on that final day as "very good." Each of the panelists was quite insistent about this point, although Todd and Tim admitted that claiming this insight was hard-fought, since it meant affirming a position that their churches and pastors steadfastly repudiated.

Angela didn't communicate much of a struggle at all; for her, it seemed, this basic insight came quickly and easily. In fact, I was under the impression that she had never put any stake whatsoever in the church's official policy: the straight white men who drew it up had no idea what they were talking about, she suggested, and neither did their Bible — which also had been crafted by straight men, she was careful to point out. Angela was the most professorial of the group. She spoke with incisive, measured deliberation, drawing upon heady academic jargon that most of us had never heard before, and probably would never hear again. Her ability to string together complex locutions with flawless precision was truly mesmerizing. My brain, still numb with food-induced coma, was unable to process all that she had to say (admittedly, at peak performance it wouldn't have managed much better). It is, unfortunately, not so much the content of her remarks that I shall remember, but her uncompromising, penetrating erudition, all packaged with charm and grace.

Second, it was clear that all felt the church was out of step with the direction society was headed and must withdraw its age-old censure of gays and lesbians if it was to have a relevant voice in the future. None of this was new or good news to the old guard, of course, whose tidy *Leave it to Beaver* worldview wasn't equipped to accommodate this sort of thing. I had heard it argued several times out on the Pamlico Sound or behind some work shed that because gay sex was pointless pleasure (that is, non-procreative pleasure), it was nothing more than mindless promiscuity, perverse self-indulgence.

The moderator then asked family members to describe how they felt when they first learned that their son, daughter, or sibling was gay, and how their perspectives on homosexuality may or may not have changed over the months or years since. On these points there was little convergence. Angela's parents said they had "suspected" she was gay since grade school, so when she finally came out at the beginning of her sophomore year, they were well prepared and took the news in stride. In fact, Angela, they said, was perplexed, even a little "miffed," by their shoulder-shrugging nonchalance. Angela broke in at this point and informed us that her parents had been reading books on the issue for years in secret, educating themselves for a journey that they believed to be "inevitable." After dealing with her "screaming rage" over their clandestine affair with literature on homosexuality, she said the family quickly reconciled, and that her parents had been entirely supportive ever since, never doubting the authenticity of her announcement, "never ever" suggesting that it was merely "a fad."

Todd wasn't quite so fortunate. Georgia and Jack agreed that they still hadn't gotten used to the idea of one of their own "going gay." "Love the sinner, hate the sin" was Georgia's mantra, first suggested by her pastor. "I'll never give up on my boy," she said several times with tears in her eyes. "He's my sweet little boy, bless his soul, and always will be." Jack remained rather tight-lipped throughout, deferring repeatedly to his mother, whose welling emotions induced a spate of heart-wrenching, though sometimes incomprehensible, ramblings. Their church, she intimated, was quite conservative and unable to accept the still-fresh revelation of Todd's sexual orientation, which left her with little support. She felt isolated, often confused, struggling desperately to somehow fit the news into her understanding of God and the ethical life. Others around me cried too as Georgia spoke.

Zack didn't have a whole lot to say. The hamlet in which he and Tim grew up saw them as "perverted freaks of nature," he said, "who some-day just better get their asses out of town," which they happily did only days after graduation. The mention of "asses" in the sanctuary didn't go over well and summoned squirms and censorious glances all around, even among some of the radicals in the room. Either Zack hadn't stepped foot in a church in decades and therefore understandably had forgot-ten basic ecclesial etiquette (like the unspoken "no-cussing-in-church" rule), or he deliberately sought to provoke the puritanical crowd. He also confessed that he never was able to make much sense of Tim's supposed "call" into the ministry and was "totally and completely freakin' relieved" when Tim finally dropped "the silliness" and got "his head screwed back on straight." Well, "not exactly straight," he added. Not many laughed, though I thought the remark was clever and deserved more accolades than it received.

During the proceedings, I tried again and again to immerse myself in my novel, but after nearly ninety minutes had passed, I hadn't completed a single page, all of which were stamped in massive I Can Read font. Their stories I found to be utterly fascinating, and I wished then that I had been more insistent about having one layperson from St. Mark's (the congrega-tion to which I had recently been appointed) accompany me to Greenville for the day. A frank though chastened and informed conversation about this issue would be much more enjoyable, I thought, than subjecting Bible stories to the stranglehold of centuries of dogma.

The moderator solicited final comments from the panelists, then opened the floor to questions or comments from the audience. The first several respondents generally began with a word of thanks to the panelists as well as a respectfully phrased question or two that sought clarification on some matter or another. It was at this point that I finally began to make some progress on my book, until an oddly familiar voice pricked my ears. I glanced over at the microphone: it was the slim, bespectacled fellow who tried in vain to prod us into a dialogue over lunch.

"Yes, um–," he said as he cleared his throat. "Well, um, I–," he stam-mered again, hampered from proceeding by some devilish tickle or bit of food. "Excuse me, um–," he managed, beginning to cough. A good Samaritan seated beside him extended a small paper cup, and the pastor downed its contents in a single gulp. After a deluge of horrific coughing and frenetic chest-pounding, he bent over and ground the back of his throat with a ferocity one might think impossible from someone so slight of frame. After several seconds of nervous silence, he raised his glasses and wiped tears from his eyes with the back of his hand. He stepped up to the microphone again. "I ... I apologize," he falsettoed, punctuated with one last emphatic hack. "I think I got it." Perhaps he was unaccustomed to the afternoon's cuisine, and this was his body's way of punishing him publicly for deviating so radically from his usual fare. Ingesting a full Southern spread does require slow, incremental habituation. "After all that, this had better be good, right?" The uproarious laughter that followed was not, it seemed to me, so much a testament to his timely humor as to the collective sense of relief felt through the room. "So, I too wish to thank you for coming. I can't wait to get hold of the DVD from our forum and show it to my congregation. Fascinating, and so helpful. Thank you so much." The pastor bowed in gratitude, knocking his forehead hard on the microphone. "Whoa, there," he said, steadying the mic stand with his hand.

Before proceeding, he raised a legal pad and scanned the first page. "So, I was jotting down a few things as you all were speaking and thought that I'd share them, for better or for worse." He then flipped back and forth between the first and second pages, as if suddenly uncertain about the relevance of what was written on page one, or perhaps uncertain about where to begin. "So, I found myself digging through the Bible for all the passages that are used to defend the church's position on homosexuality, and it occurred to me that there's really very little there." Struggling to decipher his scribble, he raised the pad closer to his eyes and squinted. "As you already know, I'm sure, the story of Sodom and Gomorrah is basically irrelevant, even though all the crazies and such on T.V. use it as the example *par excellence* of what happens to homosexuals. What the men in the story are guilty of is intending to do violence to strangers, to humiliate them. Other books in the Bible even remember the story not as a judgment on homosexuality but as a story about brutishness and inhospitality. Oh, and technically, no gay sex is even had, so they simply can't be punished for that." As he flipped to the second page, it occurred to me that I'd never heard someone around here use a French phrase in a sentence – outside the classroom, anyway. I wondered if others found it odd.

"And then," he continued, "there's the famous Romans passage, of course, but as I remember, Paul simply uses gay sex as a stereotypical example of Gentile depravity to make a larger point: everybody's sinned, absolutely everyone. It isn't even clear if Paul buys the stereotype! And, I'm betting he doesn't since he basically spends all his time with Gentiles and talks about them so fondly in his other letters. Anyway, he's certainly not prescribing Christian behavior there, so that passage isn't relevant either. Not relevant at all." A few disapproving murmurs arose from the back of the auditorium. "Oh, and I almost forgot!" he called out suddenly. "Jesus never says anything about it. And he's our go-to guy!" Several in front of me nodded approvingly. "So, here's my point: it seems like we're left with those couple laws in the Torah, and that's pretty much it!"

Jeered someone from the back row: "What's the Torah? Speak English, newbie!" The bespectacled minister swiveled back to look and smiled quizzically. I couldn't tell whether the man was razzing him in good fun about his overly academic air or really had no idea what the Torah is. Assuming that the man had a seminary education, the latter seemed almost inconceivable. The pastor, undoubtedly vexed like the rest of us, continued without addressing the rabble-rouser's remark.

"So, I was flipping through Leviticus – that beloved book we all scour on a regular basis for sermon nuggets, I'm sure – which is where the two prohibitions against gay sex are, and I began skimming for other stuff on sex and relationships. Do you all remember how bizarre this stuff is? I jotted down a few verses at random. Bear with me. I do have a point, I promise." The minister paused to survey his notes. "Okay, so here's a few other laws. You can't have sex when a woman's on her period, and if you do, you're to be killed. If you cheat on your spouse, same thing: you're to be stoned to death. Do you all remember this stuff?" Several in the audience nodded. Most, surprisingly, were attentive and seemed genuinely interested in what he had to say.

"Polygamy is perfectly fine," he continued, walking his fingers down the page as if it were a checklist, "if it suits you. And men could have a mistress or two, no problem. Having sex makes you unclean until the sun goes down. A menstruating woman is unclean for a whole week, which means that if a guy sits where she sat or touches what she touched, he becomes unclean too. You've got to marry one of your own – so, a Jew if you're a Jew, an African American if you're an African American, a Scot

63

if you're a Scot, and so on. Oh, and here's a cool one. I really like this. I'll just read it: 'If men get into a fight with one another, and the wife of one intervenes to rescue her husband from the grip of his opponent by reaching out and seizing his genitalia, you shall cut off her hand; show no pity.' Random, I know, but cool." He dropped the legal pad to one side, removed his glasses, and spoke directly to us: "My point is this: Why is it that we feel free to ignore all the rest of these sex-and-relationship laws in Leviticus but still hold the two on gay sex to be valid? It just seems totally arbitrary to me. We ought to be consistent, don't you think? Either the whole collection's valid and we start cutting off hands and hurling stones at people, or we admit that what we've got here is a bunch of really old laws that worked for a handful of Middle Eastern elders a really long time ago but don't make much sense today."

The moderator gently bent the silver ribbed microphone on his lectern forward but was preempted from speaking by the jester in the back row.

"But it's still unnatural!" the man called out with his hands cupped around his mouth. Many chuckled, including the moderator, who afterwards reached for the microphone amid a flurry of neighbor-to-neighbor chatter.

"James," he said, "do you have a question for the panelists? Or, is that pretty much it?"

"Well, I guess it's just a comment, then – an observation. And I'd be curious to see if others share my confusion here – why we isolate those two commandments and basically ignore all the rest – including, I might add, now that I think of it, all the laws that take slavery for granted and treat women like property. No questions at the moment, though."

"So, James," the moderator continued, "it seems you're among those who would disagree with our official denominational statement?"

"Well," he said, scratching his head, "I guess I'd say that using the Bible to back it up is a problem. Illogical, really. If that's going to be our stance, it seems we should just come clean and admit what the gentleman in the back row just said – that some feel it's unnatural, and that that's really all there is to it. Bringing the Bible or even God into it seems a little disingenuous to me. It's like someone has a gut feeling about it first and *then* goes to the Bible or invokes God to underwrite it."

An uncomfortable silence descended on the room.

"Okay then, James," interjected the puzzled moderator after some delay, "let's move on to the next person." James strode breezily to the front row and took a seat among others of his kind — thin, metrosexual, earnest. The bishop, ordinarily dead to the world when he wasn't in the spotlight, began shifting his feet back and forth and rubbing his chin with palpable agitation.

The next in line, a hefty balding man in his 50s who looked like just about everyone else in the room, said: "While I appreciate the young man's remarks, I respectfully disagree."

"Hear, hear!" someone bellowed from the back.

"It's not that I feel it first and then thumb through the Bible to back it up. It's that the Bible first tells me it's wrong, and *then* I feel it." A faint smattering of applause followed. "In that order!" he exclaimed suddenly, with his index finger raised to the heavens. "Nevertheless, I do appreciate your coming today," he said in a more restrained manner, tipping his head to the panelists, whose collective countenance now betrayed weariness and mild apprehension.

The moderator leaned into his microphone: "Bill, did you have anything else, or perhaps a question for our panelists?"

"Yeah, but it's slipped away," he replied. "I got to thinking about what the young man said and plumb forgot."

"Well, okay, let's move on down the line," said the moderator. "Thank you, Bill."

Bill sat, and the next, of similar stock, offered his opinion on the matter: "I didn't quite follow the young man all the way," he said. "Seems like suspect reasoning, if you ask me. Like a lot of fancy footwork. All I know is that it says it right there in the Bible: don't do it. Just don't do it, and if you're doing it, you'd better stop. Who are we to argue with God? You know what I mean? Rotten sinners that we are, who the heck are we to argue with the Most High?"

"You got that right!" someone said.

"Right on, brother!" added another.

"Make no mistake about it!" chimed a third.

The once-anemic line was lengthening rapidly as more and more from the crowd were finding the courage to speak their minds. The line now extended past the last row and wormed its way through a trove of carts bearing bright red hymnals and folding chairs.

"Michael, did you have anything to add, perhaps a question for our panelists?" inquired the moderator conscientiously.

"Like the good fella in front of me, I lost my train of thought when the young man was doing his thing."

"Well, okay. Samantha, the floor is yours!" One of only three women in the long line, she had emerged from the earnest cadre up front. Middle-aged, mousy, heavily permed, she reminded me of my high school librarian, whose porn-hot daughter played the lead in well over half of my teenage fantasies.

"James said he was curious to know if others share his confusion about why we keep these two laws from Leviticus and throw out the rest. Well, I for one share his confusion." A few in the crowd clapped, though with far less verve than those who had supported the first two men. "I would love to have us seriously rethink our position on this issue. So many in the church are silenced, simply because of what the Bible purportedly says. I don't pay a lick of attention to just about everything the Bible says about women, and my guess is that most of you all don't either. If I did, I certainly wouldn't be where I am today. I'd just've gotten married and had a gaggle of babies, because in the Pastoral Letters it tells us that's the only way a woman can be saved! And I'd never speak in church. Heaven forbid!" Several, mostly women, nodded enthusiastically.

"Here's how I see it," she continued. "One day, twenty or thirty years from now – though I hope it doesn't take that long – we're going to wake up and look back on this form of discrimination no differently than we do on racism or sexism. It'll be no different, and we'll be so ashamed of ourselves. The Bible was used to justify slavery and sexism, and we wonder how in God's name we did that for so long. This isn't going to be any different. Society moves, then we follow. Too often, that's how it's been. It's about time *we* move and society follows!" Some applauded raucously, others cheered – again, mostly women.

Meanwhile, more had abandoned their seats for a highly coveted place in line, which now snaked into the hallway. The dignitaries appeared uncomfortable with the direction in which the forum was headed and shot apprehensive glances at each other. The flier advertising the event had indicated that the proceedings would be complete by 3:30, at which point we might gather once more for food and fellowship in the cafeteria before going our separate ways. A few appointed to the farthest reaches of our sprawling conference faced a four-hour drive, so the planned terminus of the meeting certainly made sense. Already 3:15, the forum showed no sign of winding down of its own accord, as the luminaries no doubt had hoped.

"Thank you, Sherry," interjected the moderator over increasingly animated chatter. "The gentleman from Morehead City has the floor. Go ahead Bob!"

"I can't believe what I'm hearin'!" declared a hunched elderly man with Harry Carey frames that clung impossibly to the tip of his nose. "Never in my wildest dreams would I've imagined we'd be talking about this as if it were up for debate!" His syrupy Southern drawl, a bit more backwoods than I was accustomed to, summoned to mind a peeved, inebriated Gomer Pyle. "This issue's nonnegotiable," he continued. "It's bedrock! It's in the Bible, in spite of what the young man said, and that settles it. Case closed. The Sodomites get what they deserve."

The reference to "Sodomites" and their just deserts was not kindly received overall. Jeers and boos emanated from all corners of the auditorium. The moderator hurriedly shuttled forward as if he were going to intervene, but Bob launched back into his rant before he had a chance to redirect.

"Next thing you know we'll call a forum where we debate whether or not there's even a God!" he cried, jabbing the air with a gnarled index finger. "It's all crazy-talk from my end, just plain crazy-talk. Down right unnatural is what it is. Jesus'd be rollin' over in his grave if only he could see us now!" As the little man, whose eyes were aflame with prophetic rage, air-jabbed once more, the audience burst out laughing, and for a moment those on both sides of the aisle were of one mind, each savoring the irony of the moment. Blinkered by righteous indignation, he didn't immediately recognize the nature of his blunder. But after a few seconds more of wild laughter, the light bulb suddenly shone bright as his pursed lips splayed to a grin: "I hope y'all will forgive an old man for that one," he said. "Your day's coming too, I can promise you that."

The moderator leaned in, wiping tears from his eyes: "Oooeee, Bob! We needed that. Mercy me. Jesus rolling over in his grave!" he repeated. The laughter swelled once again. "So, Bob," he said, beginning to cough, "how 'bout you? Any questions for our panelists?"

"Naw," he said, waving his hand above his head as if shooing flies. "I ain't got nothin'. Frustration's all I got. We're losing it, folks, losing the battle to the seculars and such. We ain't got no guts no more to stand up for what's right." Bob turned abruptly and shuffled with disgust back to his chair.

The next respondent, a wizened woman with piercing brown eyes who could have passed for Bob's sister, broke in before the moderator could contain his coughing spell: "I am so glad we are doing this, Bishop Williams. This is long overdue. I have disliked our church's official policy for years now, and frankly I think it's high time to scrap it. All of it — forever! We ought to acknowledge these beautiful young people," she said with her arm outstretched toward the stage, "for who they are, not who *we* wish them to be. Have we really listened to them, I mean really listened? They tell us they really believe God made them this way, and therefore that it's something to celebrate, not something to suppress, or hide, or be ashamed of. When we just quote the Bible back at them and go on our merry way, what we're really saying is, 'You're lying to me. You're not telling the truth. If you just tried a little harder, you could be straight, *which is what you really are.*' Are you prepared to say that all three of our young panelists are liars — that *we* know what's right, what's best, and that everything they've told us is just a pack of lies? I'm not. The Bible's an old book, and it doesn't have the final word on everything. I believe the Spirit's doing something new among us, and we're too stubborn to see it." As the old woman turned to leave, cheers and whistles ignited throughout the hall. Those in favor of amending the church's policy were becoming ever more emboldened as representatives of their faction spoke out. She strode purposefully back to her seat, where she was welcomed like a ballplayer who had just knocked one out of the park.

The next in line, a tidy, suited white male who exuded the sanguine hyper-confidence of a recent seminary graduate, jumped in before the moderator could acknowledge him: "I wonder why we feel like we have to adjust our values and our sensibilities to what's going on around us," he said with the seductive polish and disarming chummy charm of a Joel Osteen. With his chin raised and shoulders arched back, he bounced lightly on his heels as he spoke, as perhaps he had seen other ministers do. "The church must retain its unique identity in tumultuous times like ours. It must remain faithful to the sacred trust handed down to us by our forbearers. God doesn't change, the Scriptures remind us. He is the same always and forever. I applaud my brothers and sisters on stage for their candor and courage, and do thank them for coming, but I just don't see how we can compromise one of our core commitments. If we do, what's next? Jesus' divinity? God's unsurpassable love and grace? Or, maybe salvation by grace alone? Where does it stop, my friends? Where does it stop?"

With poise, the young man cleared his throat for the finale, not for a moment surrendering his plastic smile: "I once knew a gay man back in seminary. Like me, he was raised in the Methodist tradition. But about midway through his education, it occurred to him that maybe the best thing to do was not to force a denomination to sacrifice its identity but to join a different group that would support him, where he could worship with others just like him, troubled by these ... these urges, these overwhelming urges. My friends, he joined the Metropolitan Community Church, where to this day they accept him for who he is, and he doesn't have to force his agenda – which reflects such a tiny minority in our churches, I might add – on other people not amenable to his peculiar orientation. I guess what I'm trying to say, friends, is this: there are other communities out there that accept gay people, but ours is not one of them. We can have respect for these communities, engage in dialogue with these communities, but we must remain true to who we are, and not cater to society's whims. The rules, the parameters, were fixed long ago, and our job is to safeguard them, to cherish them as a sacred trust that we shall bequeath – unaltered – to the next generation." The young man bounced on his heels and broadened his smile one last time before returning to his seat. Though well crafted, the monologue appeared to evoke deep hostility from the opposing side, for nearly a quarter of the contingency seated at the front of the auditorium shot up simultaneously like irate Jack-in-the-Boxes and marched to the back of the line.

Before the next respondent could begin, the bishop, no longer able to conceal his fierce perturbation, called gruffly to the moderator and informed him that the session must be brought to a close. The bedeviled moderator momentarily vacated his post at the lectern and walked over to where the bishop was seated. They exchanged words quietly. The moderator then returned and announced that we had already exceeded our allotted time and would conclude with the young man's prior remarks.

Jim Metzger

Impassioned protests from many were met by profuse and repeated apologies from the moderator. It was only with deep regret, he said, that the proceedings would have to be brought to their conclusion during such spirited and fruitful conversation. He insisted that extending the conference would inconvenience the wait staff, who had so graciously prepared a final delectable treat and were anticipating our arrival at any moment, as well as ministers who faced a long, arduous drive. Many of us, he said, no doubt still had sermons to complete, and he wished not to keep us on account of the very important duties that awaited us tomorrow morning. Before adjourning, he informed us, the bishop wanted to offer one more word of thanks to the panelists and address the whole group with a few comments of his own. As the bishop hoisted himself from his chair, several in the front few rows began imploring the luminaries on stage if we might schedule another forum and continue the discussion at a later time. The luminaries nodded in receptive "Let's-talk-about-it" fashion but remained noncommittal.

Then, as the bishop labored toward the pulpit, a most curious and unexpected thing happened: Angela stood and stormed off the stage, and her startled mother followed. The act was contagious, for after a shotgun meeting with his entourage, Todd also rose and bolted from view. The bishop wasn't immediately aware of what had transpired behind him and launched into a long-winded eulogy of the panelists and the first-rate contribution they had made this afternoon. By the time he looked back, two more had departed: Zack and Todd's brother Jack. Only Tim remained. Given the unlikelihood that all were obeying the call of nature, I could only assume that they were unhappy with how the forum had unfolded – or, possibly, with the bishop himself – and that their untimely departure was as a sign of protest. The bishop clearly didn't know how to interpret the gesture, for he cast a befuddled glance at his equally befuddled dignitaries and, after a few awkward seconds of silence, continued with the eulogy as if all of the panelists were still there. Searching whispers could be heard through the hall as the bishop shifted confidently into his grand finale.

"There is," he said, "some desire among our clergy, I understand, that we continue this conversation. If you would like to see us pursue the matter further, I would encourage you to contact your district superintendent. If they inform me that the response has been overwhelming, I will

70

put the issue before them at our next meeting and see if we can schedule something after Christmas – but only afterwards, I'm afraid. The high holy season during which we celebrate the descent of the glorious Savior into our midst is nearly upon us, and we all will have much more urgent matters to attend to. But I do want to reiterate before we adjourn, my brothers and sisters, our denomination's official position, which has remained just as it is for ... well, since its founding by Mr. Wesley over two centuries ago. The Bible does not mince words, my friends. It's crystal clear, and therefore any changes we might make would constitute a flagrant disavowal of the univocal command of Holy Scripture. Are we prepared to do that, my friends? Are we prepared to throw Scripture to the wind and genuflect before the fad *du jour*? Before we meet again, I ask you to reflect on this matter, to pray about it, to discern what's right with the assistance of the sure and steady guidance of the Holy Spirit. It is He who will lead us to the truth in the interim between Christ's ascension and return."

The bishop then invited us to stand for the benediction, which he belted with astounding vigor for a late Saturday afternoon, and afterwards we all shuffled eagerly in the direction of the donuts, which, to our pleasant surprise, were laid out neatly as far as the eye could see in those magnificent white and green Krispy Kreme boxes.

The cafeteria reverberated once again with raucous ministerial banter, booming laughter, and fraternal back slaps. By four, the boxes were picked clean, and we were left holding empty coffee cups and crumpled sugar-coated napkins, our cue that the party was over. One would never have known that we had just inhaled a fabulous Southern spread a mere three hours ago.

Hopped-up on caffeine and sucrose, we shimmied toward the front doors of the old warehouse and slid gingerly into our sun-sizzled autos. We waved and hollered as we bumped along the knobby dirt road, leaving in our wake a silty white cloud hovering above the desolate church grounds.

AT FOUR IN THE MORNING

Every Friday promptly at 4:50 P.M., the library staff would turn the overhead lights off for a second or two to remind patrons that they have ten minutes to finish up and leave the building. The flicker arrived right on cue this afternoon – not a minute late – and I frantically saved my work, gathered my books, and bound down the stairs toward the front door, where two young women behind the circulation desk were patiently awaiting my exit. The head librarian, stout with brown curly hair and oversized eyeglasses, was initially perturbed at my willingness to work right up until closing on Fridays, but she smiled at me now – now that she knew I was equally committed to guarding the sanctity of that hollowed time at week's end when we're momentarily set free of our obligations to co-workers, bosses, customers, and patrons. I wished them both a restful weekend as the aluminum bar shut slowly behind me.

The frosty winter air stilled my thoughts and reawakened my senses, dulled after hours under the incessant hum of florescent lights. My Tercel now sat alone under a large oak tree at the far end of the parking lot. I cherished these few minutes of solitude under the gray February sky, just before the sun's remaining rays vanished beneath the horizon. At no point during the week was I happier: a full day's work completed, and no responsibilities until Sunday morning.

The old four-cylinder engine turned over reluctantly, and a cloud of bluish-gray smoke burst out of the tale-pipe. I tried to exhale gently so as not to fog the windshield. Usually eager to hear the evening news, today I shut the radio off in honor of this somber, pristine winter evening. The short journey home proceeded down a gentle slope and offered several tight, enticing curves: a pleasant drive to punctuate the perfect afternoon.

I carefully guided the car onto the two thin cement strips that led to our back shed and pulled within inches of the back bumper of my wife's

Jetta, which hadn't been moved since we brought our son Adam home from the hospital. Pine needles and wet oak leaves now lay on the roof, hood, and windshield.

It was nice not to come home to an empty house, which was customary before Adam's birth. I would try to find ways to fill the time until my wife arrived home around 7:00, but we live paycheck to paycheck, and good hobbies are hard to come by without some spare cash. So, I often sat on the front porch, or lay on my bed and slept, and hoped that primetime television would have something to offer. But things were different now. Adam demanded that I stay awake until dinner.

Balancing books in both hands, I kicked the car door shut with my left foot, and our gray tabby shot out of the azalea bushes that flanked the side of the house and jumped onto the front porch. He shook as much water from his fur as he could and, still groggy yet hopeful that warm table scraps would soon be on their way, happily pranced up to me. I knelt down and stroked the back of his head, and he began to cry, perhaps cold, certainly hungry. I opened the door, set my laptop on the dinning room table, and walked into the brightly lit family room where April was nursing Adam. She looked up slowly. Her hair was still pulled back in a clip, and she was dressed in the same worn-out sweats and flannel shirt she had on when I left earlier that morning.

"How was your day?" she asked. "Did you finish up your sermon?"

"All finished. Has Adam been good today?"

"Not too bad. Only two screaming spells."

"What do you want to eat tonight? Can I pick up a pizza or something?"

"Not in the mood. We've got spaghetti, leftover soup from last night, some chicken in the freezer."

I kicked off my tennis shoes and skated along the rickety floor boards into the back bedroom. On a brass hook on the wall next to the bed hung this year's winter lounging clothes: black fleece pants and a green hoodie.

After placing a pot of water on the front burner of the stove, I sat down at the dinning room table and thumbed through the day's mail: several catalogues full of cost prohibitive merchandise, a college alumni magazine, and another statement from BlueCross BlueShield – this one detailing what we were to pay on Adam's circumcision. I carelessly tossed the statement on a nearby end table with the others and walked back into the kitchen.

The water was beginning to boil – as was, I soon discovered, Adam's temper. I could hear him snorting and whimpering in the next room. I peered over the stove into the family room as I broke the noodles in half and dropped them into the rumbling pot. All I could see were April's knees and Adam's oversized head angrily bobbing back and forth at her breast. Within a matter of seconds, the snort and whimper were displaced by a full-on wail. Feeding time was over. It would be at least another fifteen or so minutes before April could try nursing again.

Adam's crying continued to intensify as I gazed into the bubbling water below. Regular cries soon gave way to the "silent" cry – a momentary reprieve for adult ears, but Adam's writhing torso, deep red face, and swollen veins around the temple and forehead foreshadowed what was to come: a series of sharp, piercing screams. When Adam reaches this state, there is nothing either of us can do but try to make him comfortable and let the tantrum run its course. Although April was patient with him during these fits, I could no longer remain in the same room. The onset of a crying spell seemed to tap a reservoir of anger of which I was previously unaware, and at times I treated him far too roughly, often oblivious to the enormous physical difference between us. I focused on the dancing noodles below and resisted my impulse to "help" April calm Adam.

I opened a few cabinet doors and found a jar of spaghetti sauce. The glass cracked as I turned the cap. Whatever sauce we didn't use this evening would have to go into a Tupperware container.

April often ate her meals cold now, and we almost always ate in separate rooms. I set a plate of spaghetti and a glass of water in front of her and took mine outside on the porch, where darkness and the blustery February wind welcomed me. I sat on the top step of the porch and gobbled down as much spaghetti as possible before it cooled completely.

I gazed far up into the night sky, as far away from my present as I could. Possibility, a feeling once savored during so many past winter evenings, eluded me now. I felt trapped. The future no longer intrigued or inspired. People once said I could do anything if I put my mind to it. They lied. With a bachelor's degree and two master's degrees, I find myself at thirty-five years of age working three absurdly low-paying jobs, none of them interesting. From 8:30 – 12:30, I tutored high school kids whom the public school system had either expelled or quietly asked to leave; from 1:30 – 4:30, I performed basic maintenance duties for a large veterinarian clinic downtown; and on Fridays, I prepared a worship service (including the sermon) for a rural congregation of about thirty elderly members. None of the jobs paid over ten dollars an hour, and none lived up to the high expectations for which I once hoped. I looked forward to only two aspects of my week: long lunches at the Chik-Filet across town, and Fridays at Columbus State University's library preparing for Sunday morning. Oddly, I didn't actually enjoy leading the service, only the eight hours locked in one of many private upper rooms on the second floor of the library, far away from a life that increasingly made me tired.

I was shivering, and it appeared that Adam's crying had ceased, so I left the remnants of my spaghetti on the corner of the porch for our tabby and went back inside. I found Adam once again at April's breast. Her spaghetti untouched and her glass of water still full, she appeared to be completely absorbed in the task at hand. Her gaze remained fixed on Adam as I walked past them both into the kitchen.

I cleaned up and lazily wandered around the house until finally settling on an evening in front of the television on the couch. Adam's eyes were now closed, and he appeared to be nearing the end of his dinner. As I reached for the remote, he raised his right arm and pushed firmly against April's chest, violently breaking his suction with a resolute pop. His eyes were glazed, his body limp. April picked him up and set him in the bouncy chair next to the couch and reached for the now cold mound of noodles and tomato sauce on the coffee table.

I tossed the remote into the corner of the couch and knelt down in front of Adam, eager to take advantage of that brief window before the irresistibly adorable morphed into the perfectly monstrous. As Adam's post-feeding grogginess wore-off, his eyes began darting feverishly around the family room. His feet jerked erratically up and down, and his arms circled wildly above his head. His vocal cords, usually the instrument of an intolerable cacophony of shrieks and cries, now produced soothing coos and mild grunts.

April finished what she could of her dinner and stretched out on the couch for a nap. Adam continued to take in as much as he could of our family room; his flexible neck permitted his eyes well over 180 degrees of coverage. When tired of scanning the room, he would fix his gaze, often with eyes crossed, on his ever-moving hands. I watched in delight, taking only the shallowest of breaths. Would this last for seconds, minutes, or perhaps even a half hour? I grabbed the pacifier from the coffee table and waited patiently.

Pleasant coos were soon interspersed with grimaces and feeble whimpers. His grunts, initially benign, began to signal irritability, then anger. Within just a few minutes, Adam had sped through his warm-up of snorts and whimpers and moved on to a full wail. The pacifier proved ineffective. I gently lifted him up and carried him around the house, bouncing up and down rhythmically with each step, but his body grew ever more rigid, and his eyes eventually vanished behind narrowing lids and a river of tears. I desperately wanted to soothe him so April could get some much-needed — and well-deserved — rest, so I walked outside, hoping the cold air would jolt him out of his frenzy, but it only irritated him more. My nerves nearly frayed, I walked quickly to the back room and deposited Adam's writhing body in the bassinet. April hated that I would give only five or ten minutes to consoling him before sticking him in his bassinet and shutting the door to the nursery, but it was the best thing for Adam and for me.

Still sprawled out on the couch, April appeared to be sleeping. I rushed outside to soak up the crisp winter air and nurse my guilt. The tall billowy clouds had galloped eastward, and wispy cirrus formations now blanketed the sky. A sliver of the moon occasionally shone bright between the gaps of the passing clouds. I resolved not to go back inside until the crying had ceased — either of its own or in response to April's soothing gestures — and sat down next to the plate of petrified spaghetti, calling again to our tabby. The chilling wind and the darkness once again comforted me. I felt small and alone, yet very much a part of the universe. Mounting bills, unfulfilling jobs, and an inconsolable baby seemed insignificant under the vast majestic night sky. I wished that I would not have to go back inside, but that the universe would rescind its offer of life and swallow me whole.

The wind was growing stronger, and the mild chill that soothed had become an uncomfortable shiver. I picked up the plate of spaghetti and gently tapped it against the side of the porch. The noodles dropped onto a soft bed of pine needles. Intolerably cold, I cautiously cracked open the front door. All was silent. April was still asleep on the couch, and Adam had apparently worn himself out. I tip-toed toward the nursery, opened the door, and peered into the bassinet. Adam was sound asleep. His arms were stretched out above his head, and two small puddles of tears lay suspended between the bridge of his nose and his eye lids. I reached for a burp cloth and wiped away the moisture. He was so beautiful. I wondered if, somewhere deep within his unconscious, he would remember how I refused to console him.

Meticulously sidestepping the creaky spots in the sixty year-old hardwood floor, I made my way out with the help of a night light positioned just above the baseboard. The slope of the old house carried the door to within about one inch of the frame without my prompting it – just enough to keep our noise out and allow Adam's nighttime whimpers to reach the master bedroom. I made my way into the family room. I didn't have the heart to wake April, so I covered her with a blanket, set a pillow just within her reach, and turned off the light. A stand-by light from the DVD player and the moon's faint glow were all that illuminated the room.

The frayed cotton sheets were ice-cold, and the comforter was uncomfortably heavy. Once again, April was absent from my side. But I was happy that the house was silent. There was only the occasional rustling outside – our tabby, perhaps, or a squirrel digging in the leaves. I never glanced at the clock on the nightstand, but from the time I pulled the covers back, it couldn't have been more than five or six minutes before I dozed off.

At four in the morning, I was abruptly awakened by a series of staccato-like shrieks. I rolled over and noticed that April's side of the bed was still vacant, so I grabbed my fleece pants and sweatshirt and stumbled toward the nursery, cursing repeatedly. In the intervening hours since putting him to bed, Adam seemed to have discovered how to muster a little more air behind his diaphragm, for his cry was unusually shrill. I slowly worked a pacifier into his mouth and gently rubbed his stomach, hoping that April would soon be roused and relieve me of the early morning feeding. I went out to see if she was at least aware of what was happening. Usually sensitive to Adam's cries, she appeared to be oblivious to them now. She lay motionless, curled up in the fetal position under the blanket, with the pillow I had left for her now beneath her head.

I waited there for a minute or so to see if she would stir. Was she utterly exhausted, or was she feigning sleep in order to make me take care of this most unpleasant task? I grew increasingly irritable as I considered this possibility. I shuffled back to the nursery and tried once again to entice Adam to accept the pacifier, at least until I could prepare some formula. But with each attempt, he angrily thrust his head from side to side, and the pacifier rolled down his cheek, settling in the crevice between his neck and collar bone. After four tries, I threw the pacifier down on the changing table and jogged toward the kitchen. April, I noticed, still hadn't moved.

Two scoops of formula, four ounces of tap water, a few firm shakes, and I rushed back to Adam's side. I cradled his rigid writhing body like a football and sat down in the rocker. Adam resisted the rubber nipple at first, and formula dribbled down his chin into the folds of his neck. He finally managed two or three sucks, but then reeled back and let out several piercing screams. Again I tried – this time more firmly – to force the nipple into his mouth, and again he revolted, thrashing his head back and forth. I dropped the bottle in the bassinet and glared at him. His arms were flailing wildly about, and his feet pounded the inside of the rocker.

Suddenly, I wrapped my hands around his chest, stood him upright on my thighs, and gave him one firm shake. Adam's head snapped back and the room immediately became silent. His rigidity had vanished: he hung limp like a rag doll in my hands. My eyes scanned the nursery anxiously. I suddenly felt hot and lay Adam down on my lap. My hands were cold and wet, and my heart was thumping violently against the inside of my ribs. I looked down at Adam. He was so still, so peaceful, so exquisitely beautiful. Trembling, I stood up and carefully laid him in his bassinet. I pulled the blankets up to his neck and gently tucked him in, then bent down and kissed his forehead, wet with perspiration. I carried the bottle into the kitchen and placed it on the top shelf of the refrigerator. April was snoring in the next room.

I grabbed my coat and keys off the dining room table and opened the front door. The moon was now concealed behind a vast sea of tall menacing clouds moving rapidly across the sky. The darkness was oppressive, and the sting of the February wind felt unpleasant on my bare arms and face.

I was scared.

THE TARGET

"*W*^{*hy have you made me your target?*}" – Job

Even as I write these words, I can hear it, clawing at the bare cedar planks outside my bedroom window, succeeding occasionally in prying loose hunks of damp cool moss and splintered wood, and roving with monomaniacal resolve around the decrepit old house in search of some structural vulnerability it might exploit. Possessed of a malefic steely gaze (or so I imagine), it will pace, scrape, and snarl until it has its way, and there is nothing one might do to stop it. So I wait, trembling, searching for the courage to face my enemy. And I write, because it is time to set the record straight, before she claims her carrion and puts an end to the matter, as I wished she would have done long ago.

I am an ordinary, decent man: polite, helpful, unassuming to a fault, satisfied with the barest of pleasures, generally amicable, never rude – uninteresting, to be sure, but just the kind of fellow one wants to do her taxes or check his blood pressure. Or so I was, until a blue jay landed on my shoulder sixteen months ago today, rammed its beak into my temple, defecated, and flew away.

Now, I am a ridiculous man: buffeted by sundry fears, caged by intractable neuroses, socked by bouts of punishing rage, bled dry of desire. Surely something lives here – blood lurches through me, neurons fire, retinas and ear drums dutifully process stimuli, bowels suck nutrients from whatever bit of animal or vegetable passes through – yet I would hesitate to call it "I." Whatever "I" may have been is now eclipsed by a motley and sinister host, each vying for its share of this battered flesh. Despair's untiring, brawny grip has staked the largest claim and rendered it all so unfeeling. But many others assert their dominance from time to time too, rage among them. Though she stays only a short while, she is welcome, for at least I feel something when she is around.

Jim Metzger

I didn't make much of the blue jay's descent at the time. After all, she may have mistaken the color or peculiar curl of my unruly hair for some savory treat, and birds do defecate about as often as a man breathes. But about a week later, while eating an apple beneath a willow tree outside the sleepy office where I once worked, a squirrel mounted my trousers and plunged its teeth into my buttock. And there it dangled, limp, its tiny jaws locked onto searing flesh. I gyrated and swatted wildly without success, until an officemate spotted me from his cubicle and dashed to my side, laughing hysterically the whole way (as I too would have had it been anyone else's bum but mine). Bravely, he clasped his big gnarled unionized hands about the rodent's noggin, pried apart its blood-soaked mandibles, and hurled it into the bushes, where it fell to the turf and scurried out of sight. Aghast, we looked at one another, then burst out laughing – though he far more freely than I.

The incident eventually caught the attention of our co-workers, all women, none of whom found a trace of humor in the attack. Although grateful for their solicitude, to have all five staring and poking curiously at the wound was unbearably humiliating.

"You could be foaming at the mouth and tearing up the place tomorrow morning," cautioned one. "Happened to my uncle. I'll tell you what, he got the rabies something fierce, and he ain't never been right since. Cuzza that dang coon, he spends his days on his mama's porch spittin seeds in a pickle bucket and cursin his mangy little mutt."

The women said they'd cover my appointments that afternoon, so Bill, still tickled by the whole affair, drove me to the ER. He had a grand time relaying the story of my misfortune to the staff. By the time we saw the doctor, Bill's account had become fancifully embellished: the squirrel, once merely "loony," had become a diabolical miscreant who carefully staged the attack from afar and ferociously "ground his little chompers" into my bum, thrashing his head back and forth "like a great white locked on a seal." The doctor and I both got a kick out of Bill's animated retelling – though the doctor far more than me. It was my ass, after all, that throbbed horribly and lay exposed for all the world to see. I had always found it curious that Bill didn't leave while the doctor sutured the wound, or that he was never asked to step out. Like two frat-boys they were, ogling the bloodied bare bum, yukking it up the whole time. In addition to the four stitches that held in place a flap of mauled derma, I received rabies and tetanus shots, as well as a week's supply of antibiotics. "Just to be on the safe side," my suturist said with a smirk.

The pain really wasn't so bad. But I couldn't sit at all for the first few days, so I took some time away from work and strolled aimlessly though town, stopping here and there for a bite to eat or to peruse the shopkeepers' wares. Walking, the doctor assured me, would encourage blood-flow to the area and expedite healing. Much of both days, however, was spent meandering through our two public parks, which were in full bloom and overrun with delirious schoolchildren on spring break. I loved then to watch kids play, as it reminded me of my own fortunate youth, unencumbered by any thought for the future. Everything took place in the moment, and the future, when acknowledged at all, was simply a vast stretch of luminous possibility, a vague feeling that things would only get even better. Had I known what lay in store! It is right, I think, that none of us has the slightest clue about the future, for if we did, I for one would have been paralyzed with dread and sat life out. Or, perhaps I wouldn't have believed such gloomy prophecy and proceeded on my merry way. I do not know.

I fear that the beast, whatever it is, has finally found its vulnerability. It has been tearing unceasingly at a single spot outside the family room, where the chimney's crumbling masonry edges the cedar planks. I know the spot well: there is a small jagged hole in the rotting wood about the size of a cantaloupe where families of rabbits or mice have reared offspring in years past. I've been meaning to fill it, but I'd always enjoyed discovering that some furry little critter had taken up residence there in the spring. Maybe tonight I shall pay for my procrastination. I don't want to know how big the hole is — not yet, anyway. There's still too much to tell.

I should say, if you haven't guessed already, that I rather enjoyed my life. The job I'd held since graduating from college was a simple one, but I felt as if I was contributing in some way, which at the end of the day was what mattered most to me. To friends and acquaintances alike, I was "the tax-man." Even late winter and early spring, when harried townspeople would file in with piles of soiled documents and crumpled receipts, anxious they may yet owe Uncle Sam a month or two of pay, my co-workers' unceasing good humor eased the burden considerably. Of course, to see that faint smile of relief spread across my clients' pinched, haggard faces after learning of a few unanticipated credits or deductions helped too. Admittedly, there were a handful whose habitual procrastination and intractable disorganization grated on me fiercely, especially as mid-April approached, but it felt a worthwhile and meaningful endeavor overall.

While my job was mildly pleasurable most days, and at least bearable on the odd bad day, my private life was simply magnificent. I had always lived alone, which is likely why I enjoyed my life so: I was free to do what I wanted, when I wanted, no questions asked. And, although our town is small, undistinguished by industry or educational institution, we do have a vibrant community of artists and young organic farmers. But most importantly, the people here are uncommonly friendly, though I can't really explain why. It seems that a majority still attend our churches and find some benefit from the noble fictions spun from our pulpits, but we do so without taking the whole affair too seriously. We gratefully receive a little metaphysical solace, but without any of the hard certainty that seems to burden many of the religious – a fine balance in the modern era, I think.

Just as my temple and buttock were returning to equilibrium, another of Nature's former friends turned against me, again unprovoked. While hiking our river trail with a woman who had spent the night, a bat swooped down in its uncoordinated herky-jerky way, latched onto my Adam's apple, and pierced my jugular with its incisors. After tearing the offender loose (an egregious error, I would later learn), our eyes met for the briefest instant. His bloody mien was expressionless and inscrutable, his eyes hard and glassy. I shudder even now at the thought of that vacant inhuman stare, of those impenetrable black beads.

Unable to contain the geyser that sprung from my neck, my morning companion screamed after a runner about a quarter-mile or so ahead, who kindly turned back and dialed the dispatcher from his cell. I must have passed out after the phone call, for I remember nothing until later that evening, when I woke to a symphony of electronic beeps and a cadre of smiling nurses circled above.

"How are you feeling, Mr. Thomasi?" asked one. I tried to respond but found that my throat was immobilized by edema, adhesive, and thickly layered gauze. Another nurse gently cradled my hand and explained that surgeons had inserted a shunt and repaired the mangled artery, sealed now beneath seven stitches. "You lost an awful lot of blood, my dear," she said. "Get some rest tonight. You should be able to leave tomorrow afternoon."

I didn't. Later that evening, an infection stoked my temperature to 106 degrees and triggered several seizures, which left me in a coma for the next forty-eight hours. In all, the doctors kept me nine days. Even after returning home, it would be two weeks before my gullet was sufficiently drained of fluid so that I might swallow comfortably. I lost nearly twenty pounds. The rapid weight loss flayed so much flab from my hams that I couldn't sit on a hard surface for longer than a minute or two. On the bright side, though, my morning companion decided to see me through the ordeal. In fact, she seemed to enjoy nursing me back to health. But sensing, perhaps, a predilection to misfortune, she would depart after Nature's next broadside. Understandably, the well of sympathy for Her targets does run dry, as all wells eventually do.

My adversary outside had grown distressingly quiet, so I scampered about the house, angling for her from the windows. Unable to see any-thing, I cracked the front door. She stands now in a freshly cut meadow behind a neighbor's house, bathed in moonlight like some ancient god, tall and resolute, unshaken in her conviction that she will get what she came for. It is the only wolf I've ever seen, and she does not disappoint. Although I know she has come to play the demon, there is a sublime nobility to her that I cannot deny. But it is only a matter of time before she returns upon the breach beneath my bedroom window. The time is short: write on I must.

The fourth episode occurred within days of having recuperated some semblance of normalcy. My neck, in fact, was still stiff and tender, although I could finally eat anything to my liking. April 15th was fast approaching, and my co-workers naturally were piqued by my long absence. But I was eager to show them that I was committed to making up for lost time. So, for four consecutive days, I was the first to arrive and the last to leave, all the while foregoing lunch and working through mid-morning and mid-afternoon breaks. After several weeks of lethargy, the labor was invigorating. However, on Friday evening of that week, I was rammed from behind by a buck while retrieving the mail. My torso careened into the serrated edge of the open box, which lacerated the skin just above the abdomen and cracked two ribs. The buck and his modest harem bounced back into the woods.

The furrowed brows of the nurses suggested they doubted the authenticity of my tale, although I can't be sure. The physician on-call, too, seemed a bit reticent to accept my story. Although he may have done a fine job irrigating and stitching the wound, he did a rather poor job concealing his suspicion that I had made the whole thing up. An awkward silence hung between us throughout; he neither joked about the incident, as the doctor had after the squirrel bite, nor pressed me for further information. He merely stitched me up, issued a few commonsense instructions about caring for the laceration and fractures, and left. To this day I still wonder what he jotted in that chart of his. It is, after all, his narrative that counts. The patient's ultimately means nothing.

I missed a few more days of work, which did not bode well for me. When I returned, any sympathy my co-workers initially may have had had vanished. They were cool around me, perfunctorily relating this or that bit of information only when necessary, and without a trace of good cheer.

"I didn't want to sit at home nursing my wounds!" I wished to scream in my defense. "Do you imagine that I chose this, or that I brought it upon myself? Do you not know that I rather enjoy coming to work, and would do just about anything to turn back the clock? Can't you see that I'm miserable as hell?" But I only wished to say this.

Two days before the 15th, and long before the lacerations or cracked ribs had begun to heal, I woke to discover two tiny red puncture wounds on my lower abdomen, just above the waistline. The "bite," as it appeared to be, changed little during the first forty-eight hours and therefore was no cause for concern. But during the third day, while at the office, the two pricks blossomed into a hot pinkish welt about six inches in diameter. By dinnertime, my entire abdomen was swollen and tender to the touch, and by the time *The Late Show* was over, I was running a wicked fever. I slept that night maybe an hour at most. The remainder of the time, I gulped buckets of water while sponging my torso and forehead with diluted alcohol. In the morning, I checked myself into the ER once again, where I was whisked away on a gurney to one of two private rooms at the end of the hall. There, residents, each time a different one, uncorked a flurry of questions to which I had no good answer, and poked around roughly and aimlessly (so it seemed) on the throbbing scarlet hemisphere.

My imprecise responses frustrated them, I think, and they dallied at the foot of my bed, conversing quietly among themselves – about what, I do not know. IV's had been inserted into both arms. A nurse informed me that one of the bags was full of antibiotics, which doctors hoped would quell the infection. I asked her what they believed was responsible for the wound, and she began to say something about a "spider," or perhaps a "self-inflicted injury," when I suddenly blacked out.

Two days later, I was told, I regained consciousness. At hearing the news of my awakening, my primary care doctor visited and assured me that the antibiotics were "working magnificently," and that I should be back on my feet "in no time."

"Our best guess is that you were bitten by a poisonous spider – a brown recluse, probably – which got infected and rapidly spiraled out of control," he explained. "If it was, I've never seen anyone's body react quite like yours. That's the working theory, anyhow, though I myself have some doubts." He then scribbled hastily on his clipboard, thrust it in the direction of a nearby nurse, and bolted. I promptly fell back asleep.

When I finally returned to work, April 15th had come and gone. My colleagues were in a splendid mood, since most of what remained were files from clients who had requested an extension on their returns. However, they shared none of their buoyancy with me. My boss in particular, whose family once lived a mere stone's throw from my boyhood home and who was my constant companion during grade school, was uncommonly curt and condescending. Over lunch one afternoon, I tried in earnest to tell my side of the story to the group, but they would have none of it. Throughout the meal, a few rudely interrupted at my slightest pause, while others excused themselves to take care of some bit of frivolous business. I do not think it is unfair to say that when I was present the atmosphere was overtly hostile. I even offered to show Bill and my boss the nasty scar that was developing beneath my ribcage, but both glowered and walked away in silence. "It's the very beginning of necrosis," I told them, "a sure sign that a brown recluse got hold of me that night. It's pretty damn cool, I can promise you that!" Nothing but menacing glares all around. I had become the office pariah, a lazy good-for-nothing who had suddenly developed the habit of concocting fantastic tales to shirk responsibility. Within two weeks of my return, I was terminated with no explanation.

Jim Metzger

The assaults continued, though at accelerated pace. A few evenings after I was fired, a raccoon seized my hand between the thumb and fore-finger as I lifted the lid to one of my garbage cans. The bite not only became infected but also severed a tendon that required surgery. Even before the stitches had been removed, I was stung countless times across the face, neck, and torso by an irate posse of hornets one evening while clipping the hedges behind the house. Like the bat, it seemed they materi-alized from nowhere, and they pursued me all the way to the kitchen sink, where I was forced to murder every last one.

Days later, while repairing the crumbling brickwork that furnishes the foundation for my dilapidated home, a copperhead seized hold of my calf and clung for what seemed an unnaturally long spell, its mighty jaws locked into place by some unseen sinister force. I beat the serpent mercilessly with my trowel, then with a shovel. When it finally withdrew its ivory fangs, it paused for a moment and stared at me, uncannily composed. Afterward, it slithered slowly through the hole I'd nearly finished patching and beneath the living room floor. Would it return to finish the job, I wondered then, or was it merely in search of a cool shady spot where it might coil up and suck its few remaining gasps in peace? He would recover, I learned two months later while lying sleepless in bed, and this time return with the other calf in its crosshairs.

Need I detail the torment that followed the serpent's first bite? At its worst, the girth of my calf – its hue a dizzying patchwork of reds, blues, and purples – approximated that of a volleyball. I assure you that I am not exaggerating! There was fever, nausea, and relentless retching, but that wasn't the worst of it. The doctors bickered endlessly at the foot of my bed about whether or not to amputate the distended, gangrenous limb. At no point was I included in their deliberations. But I heard it all. In fact, I got the impression that to them I was just so much mutilated flesh they were obligated to save, at whatever cost to my quality of life. I remember pinching myself between heaves to keep from falling asleep for fear that I might wake legless in the night, and really no better off than before. Tiny raised scars still dot my abdomen and thigh as a testament to those frightful hours when my nails burrowed into the skin. Although my body weathered the toxin and battled back the subsequent infection, it would be nearly three weeks before I could walk again.

Since then, I've been bitten by a possum, two more raccoons, a black widow, a water moccasin, canines of many varieties, a stray cat, a snapping turtle, and a fox. Oddly, maybe, the possum and turtle hurt the worst, although attacks from the dogs were the most harrowing, especially since they occurred under the cover of darkness. I've also been rapped by a woodpecker, taloned by the scruff of the neck by a turkey vulture, nibbled mad by an army of chiggers, and sprayed in the peepers by a skunk. The assaults gradually increased in frequency so that I was never without some festering abscess or throbbing limb. For over a year now, I have not known a single moment of respite. The true enemy is this nerve-soaked mass of friable flesh I tote around everywhere with me, this despicable, defenseless thing.

Once, when in the ER, I gaped rudely as a small child battled its mother and the nurses over a simple throat swab. They were concerned, I suppose, that his intractable raspy cough and nasally voice were caused by a strep infection. While the staff was away, the child merely sulked and cried at first, but as the dreaded moment drew near, he became increasingly agitated and began to fist his gurney mattress.

His mother tried unsuccessfully to calm him: "Now, it only takes a second, Jeffery, and it's all over. We'll go for ice cream after," she consoled.

"I don't care!" he screamed, tears streaming down crimson cheeks. "I'm not doing it! It'll hurt just like before!" Had the nurses returned promptly with that frightfully long Q-tip, terrifying memories of past swabs would not have found time to rise up and assault the poor boy. Once released from the labyrinthine recesses of memory, they stormed his conscious mind and forbade reasoned discourse. Of course, his mother was right; the event would last but a moment and cause no lasting harm. But pitiful, impotent reason had no chance.

When the nurse finally came back, the boy seemed possessed by a demon. He emitted a horrid spate of inarticulate cries, and he thrashed violently upon the mattress. It would require the coordinated efforts of three nurses and one male resident to hold him still long enough to insert the Q-tip. Seconds later, the boy fell limp, wiped the tears from his face, and hopped off the gurney into his mother's lap. The two walked out hand-in-hand, the child excitedly rehearsing his favorite flavors, the mother fondling the tight golden locks about his ear. It was as if none of it had ever happened! But the child had added yet one more traumatic memory to the storehouse, which I can assume will only magnify the terror next time around. Oh, what a simple swab can do to the frail human psyche! Now, tell me: What chance does someone in my position have?

After galloping about my ramshackle bungalow like a thoroughbred, my foe has closed in on the front door and wedged her watery snout in the gap between the base of the door and its frame – yet one more porthole to the world I meant to seal but didn't. As it exhales, moist jets of warm air streak across the tiled entryway. Is she merely reminding me of the evening's inevitable denouement, or does she see another way in? I imagine two long arcs of incisors, drenched in saliva that pools around her gums and drips slowly to the concrete. There is not a trace of sympathy in her narrow stolid eyes, not a hint of kindness beneath that heaving breast. I close my eyes and try to stanch the fear, to quiet the tremors in my hands and feet. If only I knew when she would attack and how, or which body part she would lunge at first, perhaps I could prepare myself, and manufacture the impregnable calm of a Buddhist monk. But, who am I kidding? There is no method that might still this long-traumatized soul. Just write, and write fast!

Not long after being fired, when it dawned upon me that Nature had me under its thumb and was not about to let me go, my mind frantically began devising ways to minimize contact with Her. I am no masochist. Relentless physical pain holds no appeal for me, and I desperately wanted it to stop. So, my life became an obsessively managed regimen for avoiding commerce with other organisms. My next job, for instance, was selected primarily with this objective in view.

One morning in the local paper I noticed an ad for a "technician" to man the controls to the drawbridge that links our hamlet to the mainland. Since the bridge had been installed sixteen years ago, I can count on one hand the number of times I've seen it raised to permit the passing of some towering monstrosity, invariably the pretentious plaything of a wealthy traveler who had badly miscalculated his fuel reservoirs. It would prove a dreadfully boring task. But, that one would be shut up in a concrete bunker all day, suspended high above terra firma and its critters, held immense appeal, not only because of the protection it afforded me but also because I wouldn't ever be expected to feign good cheer. For, in the work-a-day world generally, one is supposed to carry on as if things are peachy and life is grand, a precious gift from a loving Creator. But I had lost my taste for manufacturing peachiness; the generous reservoir of hope that once buoyed me into a future unknown had vanished.

I also began parking my car mere feet from the front door to my home and to the flight of steps that escorted me to the safety of my fortified concrete cell. When shopping for groceries or whatever, I would flick on my hazards, scoot up to the entrance of the store as close as I could, and dart in and out before anyone might think to alert security. Naturally, I avoided eye contact with all and aborted any attempt at conversation to expedite the process, which meant that I might go weeks without really speaking to anyone but medical staff.

With the highest hopes, I also initiated a campaign to seal every nook and cranny that might allow creaturely access to my home. From within, the project went reasonably well, but tarrying outdoors increasingly made me skittish, and eventually triggered full-on panic attacks. So, several breaches, some large, have yet to be repaired. Early on, these and other imagined gaping holes would awaken unbearable anxiety, often late at night, as I would lie fetus-like beneath a mound of blankets, desperately trying to interpret every rustle and creak.

Furthermore, the relentless, often excruciating pain that bore down on me day after day was just about all my failing psyche could handle, so that the handful of ordinary viruses I contracted in the midst of it all typically thrust me into a whirl of despair, from which I surely would not have emerged had a loaded gun or a few bottles of antifreeze been lying around the house. To stave off this intolerable magnification of pain, I began to eliminate from my diet any foodstuffs that might introduce some villainous microbe: fresh fruits and vegetables, deli meats and cheeses, salads of all stripes. Everything I ingested had to be processed, pasteurized, or heated to the temperature of the sun. I also set a dozen or so Sam's-sized bottles of Purell around the house and in my car, which, I later learned, required a compliment of hand moisturizer to prevent my knuckles from splitting open — yet one more point of entry for one of Earth's maleficent little creatures. I tried, also, to breathe through my nose as often as I could, as I'd heard this reduces the chance of accommodating airborne viruses and bacteria, and when in close proximity to others of my kind, I held my breath for as long as I could, quaffing air only in less densely populated spaces. The insane regimen worked, but the natural outcome was a loss of ordinary social graces — and, later, desire for any social commerce whatsoever.

For the past half hour, my companion has fortified her resolve on the breach beneath the bedroom window. She no longer pauses to survey her progress or blueprint what remains but ravages the wood and mortar as if in a blind rage. She has broken through the first and most formidable layer, for the sheetrock shakes now, disintegrating under her blows, and bits of insulation lie strewn about the yard. The not-knowing-when has become a torture nearly as frightful as the physical pain itself. Perhaps I will fling open the front door, just this once, and let her have her way without any fight. There is, as I may have mentioned, never any escape, never any hope of salvation.

About midway through the ordeal, I decided to consult Father Fred, rector of the neighborhood Episcopal church, about my unusual predicament. In junior high, Fred and I were members of an inseparable cohort of malcontents who roamed the town shoving M80s into just about anything we could find, slugging shots of grain alcohol, and dumpster-diving behind Penny's for any salvageable merchandise. Despite living just blocks from each other today, I hadn't spoken to Fred since our senior year of high school, when he joined Fellowship of Christian Athletes and immediately severed ties with anyone who even looked at a girl or took the Lord's name in vain. But the doctors, increasingly incredulous and aloof in their dealings with me, were of virtually no help, and nearly every friend had deserted me. So, I really had nowhere else to turn for encouragement. Having logged hundreds of hours reflecting on matters divine and the meaning of it all, I thought he'd be able to offer some morsel of wisdom that might bear me through another week or two of this grim blighted sentience.

Father Fred offered no assistance at all. After a few awkward, terse exchanges with his phlegmatic pastoral persona, I told him about Nature's repeated broadsides, which elicited a long look of ponderous incredulity and gratuitous chin-scratching. He then leaned back, crossed a leg, and launched into an apology for the Creator's goodness, reiterating time and again his unwavering belief in a moral universe.

"There's no such thing as bad luck," he said at one point. "Everything has a reason, even difficulties like yours, which, at least on the surface, don't appear to make much sense to us. Friend, I believe God is trying to teach you something. Perhaps he is asking you to search your past and confess your sins. Or perhaps he is teaching you how to depend upon him for all your needs. I can't be sure. But, what matters most is how we bear up under adversity. Those who pass God's tests here on earth will reap an inestimable heavenly reward. Now, that's something I *can* be sure of! Friend, return to God, and he will return to you." Was I naïve to hope that years of study and reflection would yield far greater insight into the meaning of suffering than this? I nodded and thanked him. We haven't spoken since.

What I wished to tell Fred but couldn't was that the regular assaults had coerced my gaze away from the resplendent and sublime in Nature to its horrifying cruelty, to useless suffering, and to unimaginable pain. Impressed upon me indelibly was the insight that the Creator of this hard and unforgiving land could not be loving, as the Father and his ilk never tired of telling us. I was forced to acknowledge that a good and decent God would not – simply could not – create a place in which little girls are raped and killed, microbes transform the human body into a torture chamber, and entire communities are exterminated by natural disaster or genocidal impulse. Or, that if such a God had mistakenly authored these horrors, he quickly would make revisions, or simply cancel the whole affair altogether. No, if there is a God at all, he is a brute, a diabolical fellow who ought to be drug from his lair, hauled out back behind some shed, tortured unremittingly for centuries, then shot between the eyes – just the sort of punishment, I might add, that Father Fred's God has in store for those who don't believe that an unlettered Palestinian peasant who died millennia ago was his son.

I realize that the consequences of a majority of our long-battered species embracing such thoughts would be disastrous, and that the old feel-good fables peddled by our churches are far better for our mental health. But these insights are not something about which I have any choice; nor are they the product of some purely rational thought process that might have veered in a different and more positive direction by tweaking the argument here and there. No, these insights were *impressed* upon me by this bizarre world that I've come to inhabit. They were dictated mercilessly by lived experience. It is odd, I think, that God's own world would speak a word so different than the one proclaimed by his apostles. Probably most would say I'm a lunatic for believing these things, but I suppose I would say that I see clearly for the first time in my life. I do grieve the loss of the old happy Christian yarns, but once the veil is lifted, there's just no re-enchanting the world.

Regrettably, I believe that I am too far gone now to be rehabilitated: I flinch now at the faintest tap or bump; I am flogged unceasingly by my mad regimen; I am spurned by all who once cared for me. Inexplicably, Nature has tossed one of her children into the refuse heap, and there is nothing this child can do about it. The trusting, amiable, breezy fellow that once was lies buried somewhere, and some small hapless rodent sentenced to dash back and forth across the interstate has taken his place, its eyes wide with terror, its every sinew strung tight as a piano wire, its mandibles clenched shut under ceaseless psychic strain. Job's wife was right all along: her husband had run up against villainous forces over which he had no control, and whose machinations made no sense. "Curse God and die," that wise woman counseled in love. "You cannot contend." And so, unlike hardheaded pious Job, I have now resolved to heed her advice and conspire with the insensibly cruel hand that once bore and nurtured me. I will play the fool in your play no longer!

Take me, lone wolf. Do whatever you wish. Seize, thrash, tear, mince! Whatever the result, I vow not to leave this house until the wounds, whether from you alone or others yet to follow (and they will follow!), have run their course. Although you have won, know that what you are doing is not right. Know also that I do not forgive you. My resentments I proudly cradle to the grave.

This is the end of our journey, dear reader. She moans, howls, scrapes, tears; of sinister unflagging will, she will not leave until it is finished. I submit – not willingly, but defiantly, and because I simply have no choice.

PART II

GOAD'S FIRST VISIT

"*Are we to suppose that in one generation there were anthropoid apes who gave birth to the next generation of true* Homo sapiens, *and that the changes between one generation and the next were so great that the children counted in God's eyes as the bearers of immortality while their parents were 'mere animals'? Yet unless dualists are prepared to fly in the face of evolutionary biology, how can they avoid this unpalatable conclusion?*"
– Linda Badham

Irk was squatting beside a stream turning a round stone over in his hand. He was two and a half seconds from inventing the wheel when a wildebeest walked up beside him and began to speak. The invention of the wheel would wait another 5,867 years, which would add gobs of needless suffering to the poor people who scratched out a living on this planet.

"Irk," it said. Irk turned his head. "I know you, and I can see that you are a good and decent man." Irk leapt to his feet and displayed the whites of his eyes, the rot of his teeth. "I said, 'I know you and–'"

"I heard you," said Irk. He looked about for an explanation.

"I have come to give you a soul."

"What?" Irk scanned the outcrop to his right, the scrub to his left, and the valley behind, where lay his small village and all the people he'd ever known. His heart thumped against its cage, for he believed at that moment that he'd finally lost his marbles. You see, he was getting on in years. If it was true that he'd lost his marbles, he would be stoned to death by week's end or declared a holy man. He wanted neither.

"A soul," the wildebeest said.

"Like bottom of foot?" Irk lifted his foot and pointed to the bottom of it to clarify. After all, he was speaking to a wildebeest.

"No," said the wildebeest. "Like you'll never really die."

Irk spun around. "Who fuck with me?" he shouted. "Why fuck with me?" There was no response. The people of his village carried on with their chores, for they hadn't heard him.

"You will live forever," said the wildebeest.

"Who you?"

"God."

"Goad?" As Irk said this, he began to back slowly away. He was going to put an end to this foolishness.

"It's Gawd," said the wildebeest as it raised a hoof and gestured to its larynx. "Use the back of the throat, Irk. And open your mouth a little wider." The wildebeest demonstrated. "Gawd," it said. "Like that."

"Goad," said Irk.

"No: Gawd. Like that." The wildebeest once again pointed to its larynx.

"Goad."

The wildebeest gave up.

"I created this beautiful place. What do you think?"

"Not much," said Irk.

"But, it's quite the work of art, wouldn't you say? So well-ordered, all of its parts working together in harmony. And there's the regularity of the seasons and the tides, the abundance of so many different kinds of food, the laws of nature all—"

"Bugs eat on me," interrupted Irk. "Hot all the time. Sometimes I eat bad berries and shit all day."

"A glass half-empty sort of guy, eh?"

"What?"

"No matter. I've been away for a while, see, working on other projects, other worlds. Kind of forgot about this one for, oh, about a billion years or so. Evolution was going so slowly, you know. Nothing but blue and green slime for hundreds of millions of years. I got bored. What would you do?"

"What?" Irk swatted and killed a large black fly that his tribe had come to call Evil. It was one of several recent abstractions to enter their language, and it was one reason why God felt they were just about ready for souls.

"No matter. I think you're ready. And I wouldn't mind one bit if you came up and joined me once all this is over and done with."

"Up where?" Irk had resigned himself to the likely truth that he had lost his wits, so he now felt there was no harm in playing along.

"It's a nice place."

"You make it?"

"Of course. Who else?"

"But, you make this place too."

"Yes."

"I do not like this place so much. First wife – dead. First two sons – dead. Second wife – sick, dead soon. Mother – bite by bat, go nuts. Me – fall in hole, crack leg. Limp now. Pain in morning, when it rains. Why I want 'live forever,' as you say?"

"This is a much better place, Irk. You'll have to trust me."

"Why I trust you? You forget about us many years and make bad place. Why I trust you?"

"You don't have a choice. I'm giving you a soul and you will live forever."

"What about wife? What about kids? They 'live forever' too?"

"No. Just you and all your children from now on. They will live forever."

"I do not want it."

The wildebeest was becoming angry. "Well, you're going to get a soul whether you like it or not."

"I do not want 'live forever' with you. You make bad place, so you bad too. Go now. Leave Irk."

"It's a gift. You'll show me the proper gratitude."

"What?"

The wildebeest realized his error. He had reminded himself before adopting his avatar to keep abstractions to a minimum. The notion of "forever" alone must have been taxing enough on poor Irk.

"You should say thank you."

"No."

"Say it."

"No." Irk squatted once more before the stream and reached for stone. "How you do it, then?"

"I don't know yet. You'll have to trust me, Irk. But I can promise you that some part of you will live on. Not your flesh and bones, some other part."

"What other part? I am this!" Irk pointed to his chest, to his arms and legs, to his head. "I am 'flesh and bones,' as you say. What else am I?"

"You are more."

"You nuts."

"You are out of line."

Irk looked about for any sign of Ork or Urk, his two toothless older brothers, who never tired of playing pranks on poor Irk.

"Why now?" Irk asked. "Why ignore all else for so many years, not give them gift? Unfair, yes?"

"No. I was away on business. Detained, attending to other matters, important matters like building other worlds. You have no idea how demanding it is."

"Go away, Goad. They stone me soon."

"No matter. I will give you a soul."

After one more look around, Irk fled limping down the ridge into the valley, where all the people he'd ever known were quietly doing hard things that hurt their backs and knees. He wanted to see his wife before she died, and he wanted to see his kids before the villagers discovered that he'd lost his wits and began to hurl stones at him.

God (or Goad as the villagers would first come to know him through Irk's drunken ramblings one evening about the communal fire) gave up his avatar and returned to his heavenly home and there reconsidered his plan to give Irk a soul. He wasn't happy with Irk's reaction, especially his lack of gratitude, but he also wasn't happy with his poor grammar and small vocabulary. God thought that maybe he at least ought to wait until they started using contractions and had come up with a few more verbs. Plus, he wasn't quite sure he could pull it off. Have I bit off more than I can chew? he wondered. How in heaven's name will I ever extract from that bit of flesh something worth saving?

THE OLD WOMAN

"*The animal opens before me a depth that attracts me and is familiar to me. In a sense, I know this depth: it is my own. It is also that which is farthest removed from me ...* that which is unfathomable to me."– Georges Bataille

The old woman's thin blemished skin lumped beneath her eyes and sagged to a gizzard beneath her chin. Her small eyes, set deep in two cavernous hollows, glazed gray, obscuring the once brilliant blue irises of her youth. Her ears were large and sage-like, pulled to a droop by Earth's gravitational field, and by poorly chosen earrings. Like Mildred, Alice, Beatrice, and the other Alice across the hall, she masked the droop with a helmet of sparsing white, for she was old and felt it was the proper thing to do. To the young, I suppose, she probably looked like just about everyone else in the little brick building.

Though frail and fading fast, she wasn't quite like everyone in the home, for she was awake once, living in the world like water in water. As she rocked gently before the television, which blared an English accent that spoke authoritatively of lions and their mating habits and beamed footage of a pair copulating under a commiphora, she had a thought, one which she hadn't had for some time. That thought was of her husband, now dead, and what magnificent thing he accomplished nearly forty years ago the night she whispered to him over meatloaf and mashed potatoes, "I ... I think I would like that."

You see, they were sitting together on the couch, as they used to before the children were born and each of them began to inhabit separate worlds, watching Mutual of Omaha's *Wild Kingdom*, and a male lion – prodigiously-maned, gleaming gold in the distant sun – had just wrestled a much smaller female to the ground and rammed her mercilessly from behind until his seed was set free and her whiskered cheek, mashed up against the trunk of the tree, had begun to bleed. She couldn't believe that she'd said it and hoped her husband hadn't heard or would quietly slough it off as another of her senseless womanly remarks.

No, she never quite understood where the comment came from, for she attended church like the rest, read the Bible like the rest, knitted sweaters and baked pies like the rest, and was generally held to be a shrinking presence in the company of all, even in the company of her own family. Someone or something else had said this, she concluded finally, before uttering one other thing: "I don't want to 'have relations' or 'make love' or any of that anymore. What I want is ... is to be—" And though her nerve gave out, her husband had heard and understood the demure housewife by his side, although he said nothing at all then and merely rose and knocked the scraps of his meal in the trash and walked silently out to the shed, where he sawed wood and pounded nails and turned long screws until the sun came up. Two nights later, after the children were tucked in bed, he gently led the aproned mother of three by the hand upstairs to their connubial chambers, then thrust her up against the wall as if she were being arrested and rammed her mercilessly from behind so that picture frames fell and cracked and their youngest, Rebecca, who was sound asleep, woke and thought their little white picket-fenced house was about to be run through by a locomotive. Well, it was the first time she had ever been fucked.

Although she couldn't have said whether she felt more pleasure or pain that evening, she knew that he had accomplished a great thing, perhaps the greatest thing that he had ever accomplished, because from that moment she began to feel the wild fire of God's breath in her life, to feel his world as a consuming blaze, and to revel before the mighty forces all about that threatened to annihilate her. Although her husband never managed to replicate the act with the same beastly abandon and, being a good man, very soon wished to stop altogether – "It's plain unchristian what we're doing, Maude, and I won't have part in it any longer," he said one morning with a muffin in his right and a briefcase in his left, poised to walk out the door for work – she began to seek out the universe's rough edges and nourish an intimacy with the sacred that her people lost when they began to say that some things are good and true.

That winter, for instance, she would stride out into the quiet black woods after everyone else was asleep and traipse through the snow barefoot and nearly naked until she came to Beaver Creek, where she would wade up to her waist and stare at the white rock in the sky, then slog shivering back home, red and numb all over. In the spring, she would drive down to the flats along the reservoir after a hard rain and wade among the glassy-eyed copperheads, daring them to have a go at her soft white flesh. And in the summer, without a drop of water or sunscreen, she would slave all day bare-shouldered beneath the raging sun pulling weeds, planting shrubs, setting fence posts, trimming trees, hauling rock and railroad timbers, even digging holes and refilling them when she'd run out of things to do. At day's end, she was burnt and bone-tired, but she wanted to know her place in the universe, to know that she was powerless before it, and that it would reclaim her one day; she wanted to acquaint herself with its ways and live the rest of her life in its teeth.

And she did, until Christmas came round again and the world began to speak too often and too loudly of benevolent gods become flesh for love of humankind — Why hominids and not other critters? she wondered then, And why, for Christ's sake, only one kind of hominid? — so that her mind got scrambled and she began to think like other people, growing afraid of things generally, and of death, fear of which she had slain only months before. One night (she remembered it well), on the third Sunday of Advent, as she and her husband were wrapping pretty things to be placed under their tall tinseled tree, she seized him suddenly by the silver bells of his Christmas sweater and implored him to fuck her again so that she could regain her sanity. But, because he was a good man, he would not do it, and told her calmly to put her finger on the red ribbon and keep it there so he could finish tying the bow.

But this was all so long ago, when she, for a season, drove out the creeds and comforts of civilization and stalked the sting of the universe. Mostly, now, she was tired, although sometimes she was cranky, especially when the staff would inter fruit cocktail in the Jell-O or stick the remote when cleaning on a high ledge where she had trouble reaching it. But she was happy on this night, rocking rhythmically before the television, imbibing that regal English accent and the resplendent panoramas of the Serengeti, happy to have had the good fortune of stumbling onto a good thought. Probably there weren't too many in the little brick building who have had thoughts just like this one.

THE KITTEN

The kitten has come again just as it has for the past two months. It comes as the sun is setting and looks at the old woman through a cracked window pane. The kitten calls, and the woman turns in her wheelchair, maneuvers as quickly as she can between sofa and end table toward the room's lone window.

She has been waiting for the kitten. She has warm table scraps saved in a Styrofoam container. Meat, mostly, because she knows how much the kitten likes it. The woman likes meat too, but she likes the kitten's visits more, so she eats only the soggy green beans and the powdery mashed potatoes, drizzled in tan skinned gravy that clings to her fork. She reaches for the lever and pulls open the window and places the container on the ledge. She strokes the kitten behind the ears as it chews and purrs, and she is happy, happy as she's ever been. She has been waiting all day for the kitten.

It wasn't always this way. When the woman was young and wore heels that clicked and was busy with important matters at the office, a cat came one evening to the sliding glass door on her back porch. The cat was thin and scared, its coat patchy and unclean, its head hung low. The busy woman felt sorry for the poor cat and tore up deli meat and set it out on a paper plate beside a bowl of warm milk. The plate and bowl were licked clean in minutes, and when she went to retrieve them, she tried to pet the cat, but it recoiled at her touch. She saw there was an open wound on its front paw, a long gash on its back, a hunk missing from its ear. The cat kept coming back for deli meat, and the busy woman kept putting out a plate. The two got to know and to trust each other, and the woman felt good about doing this thing.

Then a fierce wind blew down from Canada and stayed a long while so that the cat's milk became a hockey puck and the little bits of swine grew sharp crystals that shimmered in the morning sun. The cat began to shiver and look tired and weak. It shook all the time and cried and even began to throw up its food. The busy woman noticed and began to wonder again about things like "moral responsibility" and "virtue" as she had in college. She had forgotten almost everything under the drone of the florescent lights at her office and the prattle of coworkers, as they filed papers, filled coffee cups, changed toner, and dropped coins in the snack machine, so that her brain had become a dumb slavish thing of habit.

She knew not where to begin, so her mind soon began churning out convincing rationalizations all on its own. It told her things like, "If I brought it in, I would suffer terribly because of my allergies," or "It's free to go elsewhere; it's not like I'm keeping it here against its will," or "It's only a stray; it's not like I went out and bought it or anything," or "I would take it to the vet, but surely it's only got a virus. Who can do anything about that? And then I would be stuck with a big bill, which I can't have because of student loans and the high price of gas and other things." One she took special comfort from. It went something like this: "Cats are designed to survive under the harshest conditions. That's why they have fur coats. We don't have them, so we need to come indoors when strong winds blow down from Canada. But cats are different. Their thick fur coats keep them warm." Granted, this cat's coat wasn't thick, but it was enough, her mind reasoned persuasively. Night after night, as the cat looked in shivering and crying outside the glass door, the woman's mind kept churning out many more fine rationalizations just like these.

But the woman's mind had given poor counsel, for the cat died one night curled up before the glass door, before the plate and the bowl. When the woman woke, she found the evening's meal untouched and the cat as a solid block, like something you might pull from your freezer. She was unable to disturb the hard ground with her shovel, so she wrapped the cold dead thing in plastic bags and placed it in a dumpster. That night the busy woman stood very still for a very long time as snow flakes fell and chilled her as she cried. She did this for many more evenings.

It wasn't long before this vulnerable woman fell under the spell of a certain Holiness preacher who had a certain smile and a way with words and got religion. The promise of forgiveness and a fresh start spoke to her. For the next three years, she would spend less and less time at the office as she atoned for her sin peeling carrots and potatoes in soup kitchens, stuffing boxes with sweets and toiletries for tired troops overseas, and hauling vaccines and toothbrushes to thin dusty barefooted people living their hot desperate lives in makeshift tents on the African savannahs.

When the three years had passed, she met a smashing young atheist from Cambridge in the camps who spoke passionately to her of the implausibility of the Christian narrative in an age of science and reason, of the possibility of the moral life apart from God, of the silliness of the notion of a soul, of the many unsuccessful arguments for the existence of God, and of the damning and insurmountable problem of evil—"the Achilles heel of any monotheism," he said, his hair thick and wavy, his eyes a deep blue, his hand on hers. The sex was simply fabulous, and she lost her religion.

More than anything else, though, what the young man helped her see was that three years of punishment did not erase the plain fact of the cat's death or her torment. She still cried sometimes when she thought of the cat, looking in at her through the door, crying and shaking, frosting the glass with its small wet nose, and she still felt confused by all the lies spun by her mind then and began to ask hard questions about why her mind had done that to her and why she had listened to it. Til this day, she has not stopped asking these hard questions, though she has very few answers.

No, she would not wake to find this kitten as a solid block, curled cold and lifeless before her lone window, for the busy woman with many important affairs was no longer busy but was dying and waited all day long for it to appear. The kitten made her happy as her dutiful son could not, as her born again daughter could not, as her ex-husband could not, as the underpaid staff at the nursing home could not. She had saved all her meat for the kitten and stroked its head and chin as it ate and was happy. She was dying, but she was sure this kitten would live.

HANNAH

Only three weeks into the school year, and the word went out: "Cotillion next Friday night/Moose Lodge/7:30 P.M." What's a cotillion? I wondered. Maybe more important: What's a Moose Lodge?

The cool kids arrived fashionably late in shiny caravans, dressed to the hilt, sashaying in boisterous shoals. The uncool were deposited before 7:30 by their parents in glamorless sedans, often alone, occasionally with another equally as shy, equally as clueless, both yearning for the cozy familiarity of their living rooms. Quickly they scuttled in to find others of their kind standing stiff at the outer limits of the parquet, as far as Shanghai from where the action would be. Having moved to town a few days before school began, naturally I was one of these unfortunates, abandoned on the front steps by my father, who promised to return in exactly two hours and whisk me away from entanglement in any post-Cotillion melee (otherwise, fun — thank you, Dad).

She arrived late — very late — with girls and boys who somehow knew how to dress just right, knew just what to say, when to say it, and to whom. Curiously, she alone separated from the happy horde, traced the margins of the cavernous hall, chatting freely with others not her kind. Dare I? I dared, presuming that maybe she was bicultural, gifted with the map that charted the way across the chasm.

"Will you, would you ... um, what I wanted to—?"

"Sure," she graciously interrupted, before I might have embarrassed myself further. And to the center we went — she first, I in distant, uncertain tow.

She parked us beneath the disco ball, and the DJ (God bless him) plunked down "Lady in Red." Arm's length, then, or the great big bear hug? Behind us, two couples were locked as one; in front, a boy and girl were experimenting with their tongues, groping gracelessly. The hug, I decided, it must be the hug. Round and round we went, silently, slowly, her melons mashed hard against my chest, my toes ramming hers, then squashing hers.

Jim Metzger

"Sorry," I said, twice.

"It's okay," she whispered. "You're okay."

At "I love you," we pealed apart our torsos and examined each other, closely, for the first time.

"Thanks," I managed.

"See you on Monday?" she said, smiling, ungluing the hair pressed to her cheek.

"Yes-okay," I said, glimpsing transcendence for the very first time, nearly a decade before I'd ever hear the word.

Had I an inkling who she really was, that she would later be chosen Homecoming Queen or only ever date the studliest, I would not have asked. No, I would not have ventured within fifty feet. But I didn't know any better then, oblivious to the unspoken, impermeable divide between peasants and lords, heedless of my proper place in the hierarchy. Had the kings that night declared from afar, "How dare he! How dare *she*!"? Either they forgave or forgot – probably they forgot with the assistance of spiked punch. But the lady in red had danced with me. Yes, me.

I had transferred twice, ever the misfit, never able to commit. She had done all anyone could do at the two-year college for women.

She spotted me at a restaurant one afternoon: "You're in school here, too?" she said, excited (so I thought).

"Yes," I said. "Transferred." Three weeks in, and we were lonely, me bereft of my rabble, she her queens and kings.

"State Fair's this weekend, just a few miles from my parents'," she said.

"Oh yeah?"

"You wanna come, then stay the night?" *Jesus, need you ask?*

Delirious, I had forgotten to stop by the ATM, so she paid to get us in.

"Sorry," I said.

"It's okay," she said.

But it wasn't okay. More was expected – I wasn't thirteen anymore. A magical evening, as they say – platonic, mostly, but magical still. Cow patties, pig pens, hen houses never smelled so sweet; tossing bean bags, rings, footballs never seemed so fun.

When we returned to her parents' estate — Bentley and a Carrera out front, lake out back (Who has their own *lake*?) — her mother told me: "You'll take her bedroom. How's that sound?"

"Great!" I said. "Really great!"

"We'll have fruit and oatmeal for breakfast. How's that sound?"

"Pretty good," I said.

She gave me the grand tour: bedrooms (seven); aviary (one); walk-in closets the size of my family's living room (three); home theater with stadium seating (one); hot tubs (two); study outfitted with Nazi memorabilia (one). Why had she taken me to her dad's study? Had she *forgotten* about the SS armbands, the flags emblazoned with swastikas, the model aircraft and submarines with Nazi insignia, the life-size poster of the Fuehrer, the ashen woolly uniforms, the gold-leaf sabers, the yellow documents scribbled in German? Had they over the years become as commonplace to her as a toothbrush or a pair of sandals?

No comment, either: "Here's my dad's office," she said, turning the lights on, turning the lights off. *What can this mean?* This was the girl who transgressed the racial barriers earlier and more often than anyone else, eating lunch at all-black tables, cavorting Saturday evenings with our only two black cheerleaders; who spent so much time with Jamie, a C4 quad, that we all assumed they were dating; who hung with the marching band — the marching band! — during football games. I registered for band my senior year only because I knew this was her strange habit.

We spent an hour or so beneath a brightly speckled dome, tracing the bank of the lake hand-in-hand, pausing at random for shy, slow kisses, aware all the while that mother and father might be tuning in. She was no Christian (a Dionysian by all accounts) and might have backed me against a tree, but I was a peasant, of a different species altogether, and made her parents cringe. We both got the message and respected their wishes that evening. Wish we hadn't.

On the pier, she said: "I'm taking night classes to become a realtor."
Jesus, why?

On the back porch, she said: "I take lots of medication — for pain, for imbalances."

Jim Metzger

"Oh," I said, feeling as if I hadn't yet earned bald disclosure, and unaccustomed to receiving it. The key, perhaps, to her whole uninterpretable life?

What do you mean by "pain," by "imbalances"? I wanted to ask, there on the porch, hypnotized to quiescence by the undulating reflection of the moon. Why didn't you ever drive in high school? (Your dad bought you a brand new Grand Cherokee!) Why did you ever speak to me, to Jamie? Why did you agree to become a minority Saturday evenings, mornings in the hallway, afternoons in the parking lot? What secret have you?

She lies now not twenty paces from my sister, beside a knotty oak – jungle gym for squirrels, shade for me this blistering August afternoon. What secret have you? You married a football player, I heard, who roughed you up, spat tobacco, shot any creature that moved, and drove too fast – in fact, drove you right off a cliff. What secret have you?

I'M LYING HERE

I'm lying here hooked up to this machine because my soul mate Angie struck me on the head with a meat tenderizer. The proximate cause of my being struck is that I had loudly pronounced the words Where's that goddamn lighter fluid while shutting cabinet doors with great force. But the ultimate cause is that my soul mate was born again around Thanksgiving and had had enough of my incessant blaspheming.

My soul mate isn't here right now. But Benny is. Benny is old and cranky and hooked up to a machine too. He is on the other side of this curtain screaming at Nurse Mary for putting fruit cocktail in his Jell-O. He wants Nurse Mary to take away his plate and given him new Jell-O without any fruit cocktail in it.

Mary huffs in and yanks back the curtain. She yells words then stares meanly at him. Before removing his tray she reaches under Benny's bed and bends the clear tube that brings air to this man's nostrils around her forefinger. Benny begins to wheeze a little. Mary then lets go. I see the vacant wooden cross around Mary's neck as she leaves and seem to remember that she is born again too.

If my son at this very moment were to come and ask me to dispense all my wisdom I suppose I'd say something like Don't fuck with people who've been born again. But my son's a philosopher and I know what he'd say. He'd say Dad that's a common fallacy of reasoning that we philosophers call a hasty generalization. You can't draw big conclusions like that based on such a small amount of evidence. If he were to say this he would nullify all the wisdom I now have to offer. Surely I've learned other important things in my life. But right now at this very moment that's all I can come up with.

Is life good like the bumper sticker says? Hell no. I'm suffering here without my soul mate who loves Jesus more than me. It's become pretty clear that I have not one bit of wisdom to leave the world when I'm gone. And they keep putting canned fruit in our goddamn Jello-O. Which is starting to piss me off a little too.

Jim Metzger

They should put a footnote on those bumper stickers that goes something like Life can be good for some people some of the time and that's all we're really claiming here. But we can't put a statement like that in big enough letters for other drivers to read so we had to condense it a bit.

ACKNOWLEDGEMENTS

Grateful acknowledgement is made for permission to reprint the following previously published material:

"At 4 in the Morning." *Short Story* (Society for the Study of the Short Story; Columbia: Wentworth) 12.1 (2004): 48-54.

"The Old Woman." *Bartleby Snopes: A Literary Magazine* (June, 2012).

"The Conference." Chapter 10 (abridged and revised) from *Dim: A Novel.* Washington, D.C.: Aberdeen Bay, 2011.